TWO NOVELLAS
BY YAE

After the Empire:
The Francophone World and
Postcolonial France

Series Editor
Valérie Orlando, University of Maryland

Advisory Board
Robert Bernasconi, Memphis University; Alec Hargreaves, Florida State University; Chima Korieh, Rowan University; Mildred Mortimer, University of Colorado, Boulder; Obioma Nnaemeka, Indiana University; Kamal Salhi, University of Leeds; Tracy D. Sharpley-Whiting, Vanderbilt University; Nwachukwu Frank Ukadike, Tulane University

See www.lexingtonbooks.com/series for the series description and a complete list of published titles.

Recent and Forthcoming Titles

Memory, Empire, and Postcolonialism: Legacies of French Colonialism, edited by Alec G. Hargreaves

Ouregano: A Novel, by Paule Constant, translated and annotated by Margot Miller, and introduced by Claudine Fisher

The Transparent Girl and Other Stories, by Corinna Bille, selected and translated by Monika Giacoppe and Christiane Makward

Time Signatures: Contextualizing Contemporary Francophone Autobiographical Writing from Maghreb, by Alison Rice

Breadfruit or Chestnut?: Gender Construction in the French Caribbean Novel, by Bonnie Thomas

History's Place: Nostalgia and the City in French Algerian Literature, by Seth Graebner

Collective Memory: France and the Algerian War (1954–1962), by Jo McCormack

The Other Hybrid Archipelago: Introduction to the Literatures and Cultures of the Francophone Indian Ocean, by Peter Hawkins

Rethinking Marriage in Francophone African and Caribbean Literatures, by Cécile Accilien

Two Novellas by YAE: A Moroccan in New York and Sea Drinkers, by Youssouf Amine Elalamy, translated by John Liechty

TWO NOVELLAS BY YAE

A MOROCCAN IN NEW YORK AND SEA DRINKERS

Youssouf Amine Elalamy

Translated by John Liechty

LEXINGTON BOOKS

A division of
ROWMAN & LITTLEFIELD PUBLISHERS, INC.
Lanham • Boulder • New York • Toronto • Plymouth, UK

A Moroccan in New York was originally published as *Un Marocain á New York* (Casablanca: EDDIF, 1998). *Sea Drinkers* was originally published as *Les Clandestins* (Casablanca: EDDIF, 2000).

LEXINGTON BOOKS

A division of Rowman & Littlefield Publishers, Inc.
A wholly owned subsidiary of The Rowman & Littlefield Publishing Group, Inc.
4501 Forbes Boulevard, Suite 200
Lanham, MD 20706

Estover Road
Plymouth PL6 7PY
United Kingdom

Copyright © 2008 by Lexington Books

British Library Cataloguing in Publication Information Available

Library of Congress Cataloging-in-Publication Data
Elalamy, Youssouf Amine, 1961–
  [Marocain à New York. English]
  Two novellas by YAE : A Moroccan in New York ; and Sea drinkers / Youssouf Amine Elalamy ; translated by John Liechty.
    p. cm. — (After the empire)
  ISBN-13: 978-0-7391-2559-5 (cloth : alk. paper)
  ISBN-10: 0-7391-2559-1 (cloth : alk. paper)
  ISBN-13: 978-0-7391-2560-1 (pbk. : alk. paper)
  ISBN-10: 0-7391-2560-5 (pbk. : alk. paper)
  eISBN-13: 978-0-7391-3166-4
  eISBN-10: 0-7391-3166-4
  I. Liechty, John, 1958– II. Elalamy, Youssouf Amine, 1961– Clandestins. English. III. Title. IV. Title: Moroccan in New York. V. Title: Sea drinkers.
PQ3989.2.E3613M3713 2008
843'.914–dc22   2008029455

Printed in the United States of America

♾ ™ The paper used in this publication meets the minimum requirements of American National Standard for Information Sciences—Permanence of Paper for Printed Library Materials, ANSI/NISO Z39.48-1992.

CONTENTS

SEA DRINKERS

CONTENTS

FOREWORD

S ince 1999 and the death of King Hassan II, which ended "les an-
nées de plomb" (The Lead Years, 1973–1999), Morocco has been
transformed, socio-culturally and politically. Encouraged by the more
liberal, democratic climate fostered by young King Mohammed VI,
popularly known as "M6," men and women authors, journalists, poets,
and filmmakers of French expression explore the socio-cultural and
political debates of their country while also seeking to document the
untold stories of a dark past. These men and women are presenting the
new face of Morocco as a country that is dynamic and connected to the
global economy of the twenty-first century. At the same time, they seek
to represent the obscure past of a nation's history that has never before
been told. The work of contemporary authors reflects original thematic
trajectories in literature that reveal a much more tolerant and inclusive
society. Artists and literary activists, like Youssouf Amine Elalamy,
confront the challenges posed by the globalization of the twenty-first
century as they discuss how best to transit from traditionalism to mo-
dernity within the conflicted polemics of the post–September 11 world.
Moroccans see this world as increasingly polarized between Arab/East
and U.S.-European/West. Contemporary Moroccan authors of French
expression investigate the themes of "le Nouveau Maroc" (the New Morocco), a label for a country that has become increasingly transparent
as it assesses and retells its history, politics, and culture.

Authors writing the stories of the New Morocco agree that since 1999
the country has reinvented its archaic, mysterious persona. With each

passing year, the Moroccan people question and reformulate antiquated notions about Islam, sexuality, women's roles in society, and the right to freedom of expression. Recent films, literature, and the press echo a new openness that explores the richness of a society that is multicultural and multiethnic. Today, unlike the past, the country is championing all facets of its multicultural identity—Arabophone, Berberphone, and Francophone—in order to support its cultural production.

Unlike in many other francophone regions of the world, Morocco's authors of French expression are flourishing, welcoming new members to its literary ranks every year. Since 1999, particularly women have founded a voice that is critical and dedicated to accurately documenting the transitions taking place in the country. Both male and female authors examine the repression of the Lead Years as well as explore subjects that were once taboo: imprisonment, torture, certain prohibitive aspects of traditional society, homosexuality, and women's sociopolitical enfranchisement.

YAE'S MOROCCAN HUMANISM

Youssouf Amine Elalamy, popularly referred to as "YAE" by Moroccans in the literary and artistic circles of the country, began writing in the late 1990s at the dawn of the New Morocco. His works in French include: *Un Marocain à New York* (1998), *Les Clandestins* (2000, Atlas Prize 2001), *Paris mon bled* (2002), *Le Journal de YAE* (2003), and *Miniatures* (2004). In 2006, YAE published *Tqarqib Ennab*, the first narrative ever published entirely in Moroccan dialectical Arabic.[1] In general, YAE's complete oeuvre, either as three-dimensional artwork, theater, or prose, is playful and primarily explores the quirkier side of what he calls "the Moroccan personality." The author's novels humorously depict Moroccans looking at themselves (*Miniatures*) and/or the "clash of cultures" and misunderstandings that arise when Moroccans are in the West (*Un Marocain à New York*; *Paris mon bled*).

YAE's novels and his artwork (shown in galleries and art expositions across Morocco and Europe), are both humanist and humorous in their investigation of the common denominators of life we all share. His works challenge readers to ask the question, "What does it mean to be human?" Often this question can only be answered by exploring human nature. Brandishing his humanist and humorist pen, the author explores a human continuum that has become complicated and divided by the sociopolitical and cultural polarizations of East/West, Arab/French, traditionalist/modern, secular/religious, isolationist/global, individual/collective.

Elalamy's novels and artwork (particularly *Miniatures*) reveal that literature and art can "restituer la dimension humaine d'une société" (restore the human dimension of a society). YAE contends that being respectful of what is dearly human is the key to depicting the stories of our time.[2] His work is grounded in a philosophy that portrays "the very foundations of [our] civilization[s]," while exploring our commonalities and basic human values.[3] The author's philosophy characterizes the socio-cultural themes at home and abroad that are vitally important to a society in transition. Equally important, his novels epitomize a new vision of "la Francophonie" that has come to promote the vibrancy and diversity of French speakers throughout the world. YAE's prose is a product of "la littérature monde," (world literature) characterized as "une littérature nouvelle, bruyante, colorée, métissée, qui [explique] le monde en train de naître" (a world literature . . . a new literature, loud, colored, mixed, which announces the world as it is being born).[4] His novels champion a globe that reflects the "grandes métropoles où se télescop[ent], se brass[ent], se mêl[ent] les cultures de tous les continents" (huge metropolises where cultures from all continents become confused, smash into and mix with one another).[5] Youssouf Amine Elalamy's oeuvre "is not just [occupying] a position or place, nor simply [belonging] somewhere, but rather . . . [is] both insider and outsider to the circulating ideas and values that are at issue in our society or someone else's society or the society of the other."[6] His novels allow readers to understand how Moroccans view themselves as well as others, and how we all must find the means to tackle the abject facets of our *being* in the world.

SEA DRINKERS: AS LONG AS THERE IS A HERE, THERE WILL BE AN OVER THERE

Sea Drinkers reveals the hurdles faced by those who illegally emigrate across the slim stretch of water between Morocco and Spain. The hundreds who attempt the dangerous crossing every year are known as the *harraga*, which in Arabic means "the burners." The Moroccans who embark on tiny boats must literally "burn" the bridges of their lives (their identity papers and passports), in order to clandestinely infiltrate into the countries across the water.[7] The characters depicted in YAE's *Sea Drinkers* tell the tales of those who become stateless and who, more often than not, die untimely deaths in the waters between two continents (a distance of less than fifteen miles). However Elalamy remarks that his novel is about more than just this one, fatal crossing: "Mon roman ne traite pas des immigrés clandestins mais bien des clandestins" (my novel doesn't talk about clandestine emigrants but rather people who are, in general, clandestine). He underscores the fact that those who leave do so because they are already marginalized by poverty, illiteracy, and despair in a country that offers them few means to make a living.[8] The marginalized and exploited live on the edge of *bidonvilles* (shanty towns), lost in the masses of people who cannot make ends meet in Morocco:[9] "Ce qu'il donne à comprendre, c'est que ceux qui partent n'aspirent pas à être clandestins, au contraire" (what needs to be understood is that those who leave do not aspire to be clandestine, on the contrary), what these men and women want, Elalamy explains, "c'est bel et bien sortir de la clandestinité dans laquelle ils se trouvent. Diplômés chômeurs, enfants illégitimes ou habitants de Houlioud, tous veulent être reconnus" (to emerge definitively from the clandestine state in which they find themselves. They have diplomas, are out of work, are illegitimate children or live in the Houlioud (poor district); they all want to be recognized).[10]

In February 2007, I asked Elalamy to explain why he decided to write on the subject of illegal emigration, which for me seemed out of character with regard to his other works. He stated that after seeing an article in 1998 in a Moroccan newspaper reporting on bodies washed up on the shore with no identity papers, he realized that this *fait divers* (a trivial news item) should not simply fall into the banality of the hundreds of news stories on emigration. These were real people with pasts who "autrement ne seraient pas reconnus" (otherwise would not be acknowledged) if they had not embarked on that one, fatal voyage.[11] The irony that death makes one "reconnu," at least as a victim, is a central theme in Elalamy's novel. Yet even in death, some of these people have no papers or "identités" and their bodies are rarely claimed once found on the shores of Morocco or Spain. YAE's story is constructed as a series of images—montages—of scenes that visually parade across the page. These represent a world that, although fragmented as the author points out, when put together do ultimately "restitutent une dimension humaine" (reinstate a human dimension) that would otherwise go unnoticed.[12]

Elalamy's *Sea Drinkers* compels readers to stop and acknowledge seemingly prosaic objects and people who do, indeed, have pasts. The shantytown on the edge of the sea in YAE's novel is a place where people live, make love and life. This community cannot and should not be hidden behind walls or ignored in the contemporary sociopolitical dialogues of a country in the midst of socioeconomic and political transition.[13] In order to recognize their importance in this living continuum, YAE's prose emphasizes that a worm on an apple is as beautiful as the moon shining on the water because they are all from the living world and have a stake in it.

> Let's take it again from the top.
> This is the story of twelve men and a woman. The woman is pregnant: twelve plus one makes fourteen. Fourteen characters crossing the blue in the black of night. Fifteen, with the little wooden boat. Sixteen, with the moon observing them from her blind eye. Seventeen, with the moody sea. Eighteen, with the fruit basket. Nineteen, even, counting the worm on board an apple.
> Let's take it again from the top. This is the story of a worm on board an apple in a fruit basket on a little wooden boat on a choppy sea beneath the blank look of the moon in the company of twelve men and a pregnant woman.
> From the top. This is the story of a white parasite on board a red fruit in a yellow basket on a small blue vessel on a black sea beneath a white eye in the company of thirteen gray shadows of which one, it must be remembered, is expecting a child whose color is not yet known. (148)

YAE's novel obliges readers to realize the injustice of the human condition. Why must some risk their lives to improve their lot, while others bask in comfort? His small glimpse into one night, on one beach, in one country, entreats us to contemplate another world, another possibility for a fate that, although often our neighbor's, could be, at any time, our own.

A MOROCCAN IN NEW YORK: THE GLOBAL MAN

Published in French in 1998, *A Moroccan in New York*, or MiNY for short, tells the tale of a young man seeking to make sense of two cultures which seemingly could not be more opposite yet, as he discovers, are on many levels so much the same. Autobiographical, YAE admitted to me that MiNY is the compilation of the musings of a young man on a Fulbright grant in New York in the early 1990s.[14] In particular, the work reveals a plethora of misconceptions and misunderstandings Americans have about Moroccans and, for that matter, Others, as depicted in the following U.S.-Moroccan encounter:

> I made her acquaintance one evening at the home of H. Rosenberg, eminent member of New York's International House, and first-rate tango dancer. She was a pale, sickly woman with blank eyes set in thick lids that seemed to be bearing the grief of the world.
>
> "So, you're from Morocco," she said, between nibbles of caviar and smoked salmon. "It must be tough being from a country where there's nothing to eat."
>
> Not knowing quite how to respond, I merely reminded her of the suffering apparent from the South Bronx to North Harlem. The gutted shops, the burned-out buildings, the innumerable ill-lit, cold-water tenements crammed with whole populations consumed by hunger, fear, and hopelessness; the countless panhandlers and homeless people one saw each day criss-crossing the street, or pursuing their "careers" in the subway system; the children huddled together for warmth in the carcasses of abandoned cars, too weak and weary for play. (65)

Surprisingly, YAE's diary-novel was written in Morocco, two years after he returned home. Written long before September 11 and our current, catastrophic wars in Iraq and Afghanistan, the novel depicts an America of another era. The Moroccan in New York discovers a multicultural, multiethnic, and polyglot space that is practically utopist, as it invites readers to celebrate the interconnectedness of our global society. YAE reveals what is essential in order to foster meaningful human relationships that transgress ethnic and national boundaries. A Moroccan in New York recalls the remarks of literary cultural theorist, Edward Saïd, who notes that the humanist author writes beyond "the existence of powerful ideological and national barriers." S/he steps outside her/ his borders in order to pursue a "lifelong dedication that has existed in all modern societies among scholars, artists, musicians, visionaries, and prophets to try to come to terms with the Other."[15]

A Moroccan in New York depicts the foibles and banalities as well as the positive aspects of American culture as studied from the vantage point of a Moroccan outsider. YAE tries to come to terms with the Other he confronts on a daily basis, which is often both a source of exasperation and inspiration. Although originally in French, the author's prose embraces the multilingual realities of a diverse world. He writes for the reader who is not only anglo-francophone but also "Ameroccan"—someone who, like the author, lives on the margins of many societies without embracing any particular one. The author is engulfed in "Nous York Sidi," a space he defines as somewhere between the more traditional homeland he left behind, and the chaotic, postmodern world of New York America, captured in the chapter entitled "Miss Liberty":

> I'd been living in anticipation for more than twenty years. It all started the day my teacher handed me a snapshot of an Amazon holding a torch, bearing the caption: "Liberty Lighting the World." But this was the real thing—I was on the Ferry connecting Manhattan and the Statue of Liberty, gliding slowly, the pure, still sea unravelling like a vast blue turban.
>
> Standing at the rear of the boat, I watched the city draw away, and recalled these words from Celine: "New York is a town on its feet. Our cities lie down by the rivers or the sea, stretching into the landscape, awaiting the traveller; but this one refuses to bend—it stands erect, straight and intimidating." As we pulled further from shore, the skyscrapers stood tiptoe, peering over us with their glass eyes.
>
> The drone of the engines occasionally retreated under an upsurge of voices, describing and commenting in several languages. Far from being a punishment of God, the mish-mash of tongues was soothing to my ears, and I counted myself fortunate to be on board this floating Babel. A flock of Japanese tourists suddenly swamped the back of the boat, just as suddenly assuming a statuesque rigidity, their faces hidden behind the Cyclopean eyes of their cameras. (16)

YAE's prose offers us a life model for the ideal global citizen of our time. The author does not belong to just one country, but many; and like a sponge he draws in, and soaks up, the multifaceted experiences he encounters. A *Moroccan in New York* is a novel of the "Third Space," a negotiating milieu which is a "nondetermined space" that allows an author to make connections and alliances with others, equitably and/ or "rhizomatically," as prescribed in the nomadic philosophy of Gilles Deleuze and Félix Guattari.[16] YAE's novel pulls us into a world that is both Moroccan and American—same but different—allowing us to collide, fuse, and *become* together on one vast plane. As a nomadic author, who builds bridges between the polarities of Self and Other in order to abolish the divisive gaps between *us* and *them*, YAE travels to new, uncharted territories that he discovers, in the end, are not much different from those he left behind.

> En Amérique il y a les villes riches et il y a les villes pauvres. Et puis il y a New York: une ville riche, riche d'un million de pauvres. Pour le Marocain que je suis, les mendiants qui investissent les rues de New York offrent un spectacle familier. Peut-être est-ce grâce à eux que je me sens toujours un peu chez moi, ni trop perdu, ni trop dépaysé.[17]

> (There are rich towns and there are poor towns in America. And then, there's New York—a town rich with a million poor. For a Moroccan such as myself, the beggars crowding New York's streets are nothing new. Maybe it is thanks to them that I always feel at home in New York, not too lost, not too uprooted.) (7)

Perhaps at no time in Moroccan history have writing and literary creation been so vital to founding the dialogues and intellectual discussions necessary for shaping the contours of new political practices, cultural mores, and societal trends at home and abroad. Youssouf Amine Elalamy's novels help us to understand a country to which Americans have been tied for centuries, yet to which they have paid little attention. The author depicts new literary themes from a corner of the world that is in the throes of immense transformation. His prose is vital to founding the humanist debates that will establish and engage a twenty-first century that is tolerant and inclusive, all the while, continuing to be globally connected.

Valérie Orlando
University of Maryland, College Park

NOTES

1. Publisher: Khbar Bladna, 2006.
2. Interview with Youssouf Elalamy, Rabat, Morocco, 21 February 2007.
3. Jens Zimmerman, "Quo Vadis?: Literary Theory Beyond Postmodernism." *Christianity and Literature* (Vol. 53. No. 4, Summer 2004: 495–519): 500.
4. Michel Le Bris and Jean Rouad, Eds., *Pour une littérature monde* (Paris: Gallimard, 2007): 32.

5. Le Bris, 32.

6. Edward Said, *Humanism and Democratic Criticism* (New York: Columbia University Press, 2004): 76.

7. Khalid Zekri, *Fictions du réel. Modernité romanesque et écriture du réel au Maroc: 1990–2006* (Paris: L'Harmattan, 2006): 66–67.

8. "Un drôle de poisson: Les Clandestins de Youssouf Amine," Découverte. 21 Oct. 2001. http:// www.afrik.com/decouverte.

9. A Human Rights Watch report on Moroccan clandestine emigration to Spain notes that many of these emigrants are children under the age of eighteen. "All too often they find violence, discrimination, and a dangerous life on the streets of unfamiliar cities. When apprehended in Spain they may be beaten by police and then placed in overcrowded, unsanitary residential centers. Some are arbitrarily refused admission to residential centers. The residential centers often deny them the health and education benefits guaranteed them by Spanish law; in these centers, children may be subjected to abuse by other children and the staff entrusted with their care. If they are unlucky, they may be expelled to Morocco, where many are beaten by Moroccan police and eventually turned loose to fend for themselves." "Spain and Morocco, Nowhere to Turn: State Abuses of Unaccompanied Migrant Children by Spain and Morocco," *Human Rights Watch* (Vol. 14, No. 3 (D), May 2002), 1.

10. "Un drôle de poisson" www.afrik.com/decouverte, n.p. "Houlioud" is pronounced "Hollywood," which, in the Moroccan context, is an antonym for the glitzy neighborhoods the title connotes. Elalamy is also alluding to an exceedingly wealthy community outside Casablanca ironically called "California."

11. Interview with Elalamy, Feb. 21, 2007.

12. Interview, Feb. 21, 2007.

13. During Hassan II's time numerous walls were built around shantytowns across Morocco in order to hide them from the view of tourists who come every year to enjoy the beaches. Since 1999, new King Mohamed VI has launched several initiatives to tear down these walls and build affordable housing for the desperately poor.

14. Based on our conversations at the University of Maryland, College Park, in November 2007 during the colloquium "Maghreb at the Crossroads," in which YAE participated as a guest speaker.

15. Edward Saïd, *Reflections on Exile and Other Essays*. Cambridge, Mass.: Harvard University Press, 3rd Printing, 2002: 583.

16. See: Valérie Orlando's *Nomadic Voices of Exile: Feminine Identity in Francophone Writing of the Maghreb* (Ohio University Press, 1999), which is theoretically based on the philosophy of Gilles Deleuze and Félix Guattari's *Mille Plateaux* (Paris: Editions Minuit, 1980) and Homi K. Bhabha's *The Location of Culture* (Routledge, 1994).

17. http://www.bibliomonde.com/livre/marocain-new-york-un-472.html.

A MOROCCAN IN NEW YORK

Youssouf Amine Elalamy

Translated from the French by John Liechty

1

ANA MORENA

Once I arrived in New York, my first task was to get a roof over my head—the next, to find a good hairdresser. So, after checking into International House, I went to a small styling salon I'd noticed on the corner, called "Twirls." Jocelyn, the manager, and her two assistants, Clara and Isabel (an incomparable shampooist), were all of Dominican origin, like most residents of that part of Spanish Harlem. Besides being witty and attractive, they combined to give me just the look I wanted. We hit it off from the start, and once monthly thereafter, I returned to Twirls for a half hour of blessed repose. Jocelyn was divorced, the mother of a little girl. Her ex-husband passed by the salon often. I regularly observed them paired in the mirror, kissing with the languorous ardour of newlyweds. Once we'd become familiar enough, I asked Jocelyn what was up, and was given this agreeable reply: "Pedro and I are divorced for better or for worse."

But this isn't about Pedro, or Jocelyn, or Clara, or even Isabel—if I mention these names, it is only to introduce Ana Morena. Our paths had crossed at Twirls on various occasions, but as I always seemed to be leaving just as Ana Morena was arriving (or was it the other way round?), we'd had no chance to get acquainted. This time, however, we were the only customers in the place, and in the space of a haircut, Ana Morena and I got closer than we would ever come again.

She was perhaps thirty years old, plump, lively and extremely seductive, in spite of a sunburn. My presence didn't seem to bother her in the least, and using a Spanish-English blend, she bared her soul with that facility for openness Latin people are reputed to have. She spoke rapidly, as if her days were numbered, as if she had to get her whole life story out before the haircut was over. Thus it was that in fifteen minutes I came to know the names and addresses of her two ex-husbands, the size of their underwear (one took medium, the other extra-large), and their favourite sexual positions. She listed the lovers she had had since that first-ever encounter on the beach—one that had left a salt taste in her mouth. I learned their phone and social security numbers, their sizes (shoe sizes too), and the price of the purple panties that drove them wild, and which she periodically found on sale.

There'd been many men in Ana Morena's life, but she had not managed to hang on to one. Several had left her, only to end up in prison, or, as in the case of her first husband, had been driven to suicide.

As a baby, Ana Morena had made more noise than the entire nursery, and wrecked her father's sleep. One full-moon night, worn down by insomnia and the congenital sarcasm of his wife, Manuela, he'd flown the conjugal nest, never to return.

At eight months, Ana bit her brother relentlessly (she had four teeth then), and a few years later, took the pornographic pictures he'd stashed under his bed, and sold them outside high schools for 50 cents apiece. Manuela found out, and Ana's brother joined the army in disgrace.

At fourteen, Ana carried on an intimate relationship with a city official in his forties, which led to a charge of statutory rape and forever ruined his ambitions to be elected to the city council. At least he was able to follow the election from his cell, thanks to the transistor radio Ana had slipped in by bribing a guard.

At eighteen, she met Emilio at the Copacabana. He was salsa dancing like a young god, and could not, she'd reckoned, perform otherwise in bed. After their first dance, they pledged eternal commitment, and Emilio improvised a ring from a lock of hair plucked from his own head. They left on the wedding trip the very next week, tested their wings in the Alps, and tried again in Venice for a few days. Then Verona, Florence, and Pisa in quick succession. It was there in Pisa, facing the famous leaning tower that Ana Morena was forced to admit the truth: Emilio the salsa god, didn't have a clue how to dance in bed.

Later, after they were checked into a little hotel in the capital, she took advantage of her husband's temporary absence to challenge the Roman receptionist to a duel. Emilio returned sooner than expected, surprising them on the field of battle in precisely the same combat position his wife had been urging him to assume the night before. Unable to endure the pain, Emilio backed from the room without a word. He checked train schedules, and within the hour he threw himself in front of the Naples Express, derailing the train and causing the death of an adorable little chow, and ten abominable skinheads on their way to a soccer match.

Ana Morena rejected male company for a full two weeks following her return from Italy. But pressured by Nunez, the corner baker, she allowed herself to be kneaded behind the counter, and again in front of the oven, before accepting an ultimate kneading beneath the watchful eye of the Blessed Virgin. As leaving the country this time was out of the question, Ana was content to celebrate her second marriage at a small hotel in Brooklyn. There, the receptionist was a woman and besides, Nunez smelled so irresistibly of bread that Ana Morena had no intention whatsoever of letting her appetite stray.

It was not until much later the same year that Ana again yielded to temptation. This time, it must be said, she had ample cause. She was filling in behind the counter, when Mario came in for a loaf of bread—Mario her first lover, the one she'd met on the beach, the one who'd left the salt taste in her mouth. They reminisced that first experience together, and later the same morning, Mario (who's built an impressive reputation as a plumber) returned to the bakery under the pretext of checking the pipes. He slipped beneath Ana Morena's sheets with every intention of unblocking her drain.

Like something from a soap opera, Nunez got back early, surprising the lovers in each other's arms. Mad with rage, he flung the present he'd brought his wife across the room—a Singer sewing machine, the model she'd always dreamed about. He then proceeded to the kitchen, where he seized the first sharp object at hand, shooting a glance to where Ana sat motionless, downcast eyes on the bed. With one hand, he lifted the young man prostrated at his feet, and with the other cleanly severed his penis, which he brandished on high like some spoil of war. Mario managed a few steps back, before sinking to the bed. With the eyes of a trapped animal, he watched the blood drain from his body.

To the numerous women who came to her support in those difficult times, Mario's mother, Fernanda Maria Sanchez, repeated the same words: "He was always dreaming about meat." As they evoked the amours of the past, Mario had mentioned to Ana Morena the bad dream he'd had the night before, that had made him bolt upright, and run to clear his throat, rinse his mouth, and clean his teeth. Mario dreamed he had been eating an entire lamb all to himself—a lamb roasted in butter, crisp and golden, and seasoned to perfection. Between mouthfuls, he even fancied he could hear Fernanda Maria Sanchez whispering a caution in his ear: "Anyone who sees himself eating meat in his sleep can expect big trouble."

He had briefly grasped the dream's meaning as he watched Ana Morena whip her dress to her thighs and offer up a feast. A few hours later, his body spattered with blood, Mario left the world as he'd come in, buck-naked and without his consent.

Nunez the baker, meanwhile, sank back in a chair, totally drained himself. Pointing a finger at Ana Morena, he solemnly vowed never again to share his bed with another woman; or as he put it, "to never again dip his bread in another's soup." Nunez didn't realise how prophetic these words were, till he'd spent a good deal of time in prison, where the soup he'd referred to was not on the menu.

Ana Morena's world was turned upside down. In the space of a minute, she'd lost a husband, a lover, and a brand new sewing machine. Today though, that was all ancient history. Since meeting Armando, her latest conquest, fate seemed to be taking a turn for the better. Ana Morena launched into this latest chapter of her life story, but I was no longer following, as Jocelyn had begun to massage my scalp with her long, capable fingers.

I took care of the bill, cast a last glance at Ana Morena, and gave a kiss to Jocelyn, Clara, and the ravishing Isabel. I left Twirls Salon under grey skies, with the sense that something had been left unfinished. Even if I lived to a ripe old age, I would never know whether Armando preferred the missionary position, or the one Ana Morena referred to as "horse and rider."

2

BLESSED ARE THE COMMUNICATORS

There are rich towns and there are poor towns in America. And then, there's New York—a town rich with a million poor. For a Moroccan such as myself, the beggars crowding New York's streets are nothing new. Maybe it is thanks to them that I always feel at home in New York, not too lost, not too uprooted. Yet, the most striking thing about this group of people, is not its size, considerable though that may be, rather its ingenuity, its application of a singular and unpredictable intelligence that is part of the creative atmosphere of this town.

Jingling a few coins in the palm of the hand, calling out to an all-powerful God, expressing one's grievances to the point of losing one's voice, displaying a barefoot host of offspring—the genre of begging so familiar in Morocco is in danger of extinction. In New York, it is not powerlessness or misery that stirs sympathy, but audacity and imagination.

In a society devoted to entertainment, where the instantaneous is all that matters, where the stage has replaced life, the poor person had better play along. He knows it is not enough to merely solicit passers-by. Advertising has hit street level to stay, and stolen our attention. It has overrun every fence, bus stop, subway station—all places the poor once had to themselves.

In an environment of cut-throat competition, it is no longer acceptable to be both poor and a boor. To survive, it is necessary to distinguish oneself, to affirm a personality, to market a unique image, a way of talking that is yours and yours alone, to pull out of your hat some unexpected detail or scene, some unusual piece of behaviour or surprising turn of phrase that will succeed in attracting passers-by and in holding their attention. In short, it is necessary to fill one's lungs with the air of the times—that blend of oxygen, nitrogen, and advertising. The beggar has understood all this, and instead of pursuing pedestrians, has found it more in his interest to pursue the market.

On the platform at Christopher Street Station, a young man produces jazz on an instrument that is unusual, to say the least. His bass consists of a washtub, broom handle, and several strings. The people using the trains seem pleasantly surprised, and gladly toss a few coins to this master of improvisation. They react from passion, not compassion. What appeals to them is the man's intelligence, not his poverty. It is his entrepreneurial spirit, his capacity to make do with the materials at hand. In this rigidly defensive environment, this suspicious, untrusting society where one even learns to avoid looking at another person, this beggar has cracked the code and is hauling them in.

Elsewhere, just a few blocks from Macy's, a beggar thinks nothing of asking for donations to help buy a 357 Python, (the same firearm carried by New York's police force). To my astonishment, a number of bemused passers-by chuck a coin into the cup he holds in his hand. Here again, their response is not to his miserable state, but to his audacity and sense of what's going on. After all, if a million dollars a minute are spent to avoid war, why not throw in a few cents more for a moment's peace?

A bit further on, in Time Square, a beggar stands motionless, indifferent to the crowd around her. Her eyes are fixed on some imaginary point beyond time and space. A sheet of paper pinned to the statue's bust reads: "I don't move to make money." Standing within a maze of giant billboards and extravagant neons, this woman has realised that to survive one has to learn a few tricks from the ad-people—not just techniques of solicitation, or how to bend the truth a bit, but how to hit on an original formula that will make a sensation. Even the people most in hurry are powerless to resist her. They all stop, charmed by the show. And once, they've left their coins or bills, it is in appreciation for what she'd succeeded in doing where they have all failed—making money without lifting a finger.

The next evening, I decided to retrace my steps, as I still hadn't gotten enough of the show. It had rained a lot that day. In the deserted square, a body had run aground at the very spot where the statue-woman had stood the day before. There lay the face of a fallen angel, tirelessly lapped by waves of neon lights. A trickle of blood, or perhaps wine, had dried on its cheek, a message in red.

Like so many others in this city, this victim of cold and hunger and indifference had apparently run out of ideas.

3

LAST TANGO
IN NEW YORK

I wasn't sure I could dance my way out of this one. I was attending the Wednesday session on ballroom dancing offered at International House. That fateful evening, we were learning to tango, under the tutelage of the right honourable H. Rosenberg. We were to work on a few steps individually—then, at his signal, with the partner of our choice.

I spotted her in the middle of the floor—a ripe bloom, a desirable desert rose. Her generous golden bosom trembled delicately, slung in the low neckline of a dress whose pastel shades blended perfectly with her dusky complexion—a short dress that held her hips, and moulded the slight, firm arc of her belly. A pair of long, petal earrings replicated her slightest move. I noted the cross at her wrist, and two others around her neck, fancying that I saw in her a religious air, that mysterious mix of ecstasy and melancholy, of faith and desire. As Matzneff put it: "There is nothing quite so voracious as a praying mantis in bed."

Dazzled in this light, I paused to regain my bearings. She was radiant and beautiful, and not even the regulars at the Copacabana danced with such grace. There was something childlike in her as well—the charm of the bright eyes, the way she held a hand to her lips. My heart leapt with anticipation. I longed for her warm breath on my cheek, the scent of her skin, the throaty lustre of her voice. I longed for the moment when, annoyed by the old toad coming toward her to brush against her youth, she would turn gratefully to my arms. I had visions of our bodies intertwined, merging under the heat of a Latin rhythm.

I went to her as if drawn by the eyes, my mouth set in a purposive little smile. Just as I was about to ask her to dance, I found myself in the arms of another woman. Come out of nowhere, she dragged me across the floor, while I watched the blossom of my desire bob away like a rose on the tide.

Andrea was well past fifty. My face was buried in her fiery mane, now half-turned to ash. She clasped me to her breast with the intensity of a beast in rut, huskily voicing the same phrase over and over: "I've found you at last!"

Dance lessons took place after the evening meal, and Andrea's flesh was steeped in the gentle fragrance of the kitchen. Her breath was a blend of grape juice and salami, backed by a salad of chopped onions with fresh garlic-stuffed tomato. For desert there'd been a ginger tart dusted with cinnamon, at which Andrea had ritually hesitated, then devoured. I was touched by the occasional drop of sweat off her forehead, I felt the pressure of her clammy hand in my back, and everywhere smelled a troubling odour of incense. In accordance with H. Rosenberg's instructions, her grip on my hand had become so relentless that I resolved to have it seen by a specialist.

The ginger had abated, but the garlic held strong, as she said again: "At last, I've found you!"

She had been waiting more then ten years for this moment, since the day she'd gone into a little shop in Brooklyn specialising in exotic herbs, rare oil, and cosmic music. There was something of everything there for sale—Jericho roses in earthenware baskets, black candles that emitted peculiar scents, plants to work spells by, polychrome plaster Madonnas, mysterious vials of turquoise-coloured essence, and wax dolls with their sets of voodoo pins.

Behind a carved screen at the back of the store, a fortuneteller had spread a line of Tarot cards on the table, and informed Andrea that she was destined to meet her soul mate at a dance. He would be an exceptional man, nothing less than an Arabian prince, slim and tawny as a gazelle, his bottomless eyes dark as a prune dried in the desert sun.

Since that time, Andrea had frequented The Lexington and the Waldorf, as well as the humbler nightspots along Atlantic Avenue and in the Arab quarter of Queens. She'd even had a dream about this man destined to turn her life around. And when she woke, she had felt light and refreshed, and dead certain that she would live to see her moment of destiny.

Keeping her eyes closed, she could visualize her prince to the least detail. Then, years later, she spotted me on the dance floor, the radiant figure in her dream, and her happiness was complete. I was the one. I was the Arabian prince, in person. Here. Now.

Since that visit to Brooklyn, there was nothing in Andrea's life that had not been foretold. She knew she would find a curious line in the palm of my right hand. She was not put off by the way I avoided her gaze, for she'd always known that I would. She revealed the Arabic names of our two future sons. She'd even known about the mole on my lower neck, and was ravenous to get her lips on it.

I assured her, heart shattered, that I was not an Arabian prince, rather a modest Moroccan student living on a modest scholarship in a modest boarding house on 122nd Street. The news merely sharpened her appetite, as the fortuneteller had specifically stated that the man of destiny would be as well a man of modesty. I observed that the dancing had had a dizzying effect on me, that I needed a breather. This too delighted her, as she'd never dared to dream her mere presence would be enough to make my head spin. Whether attempting to express her inexpressible love, or making a simple remark, Andrea anointed me each time with a whiff of garlic that made my nostrils flit like a drunk butterfly.

I spent the entire evening in Andrea's arms, my nose smashed against her chest, where a drooping breast occasionally regarded me with a blind and withered eye. As I came up for air, I glanced over her shoulder to see one last time my goddess, vaulting about the floor like a leaf carried on the wind.

At the close of a seemingly interminable tango, a voice announced that the ball was over. Fearing the worst, Andrea eventually agreed to release me on one condition—that I would swear to see her again the following Wednesday, at the very latest, same time, same place. I swore.

I have no idea what's become of Andrea. As for me, I decided to forego the dance class. I gave up grape juice and salami. I no longer tolerate onion, tomato, cinnamon, or ginger; and I no longer listen to the tango—it smells too much like garlic.

4

HOMO HAMBURGERUS

Past midnight, in a McDonald's somewhere on the West Side. The usual anxieties, doubts, the usual questions. . . . Who am I? Where did the world come from? Did it really begin with a bang? And if so, who pushed the detonator? What is the origin of life on this planet? It is common knowledge that the ape descended from the trees, but did man really descend from the ape? And if he did, why not have just come straight down from the trees? Vertigo perhaps? Obesity? A bad case of sciatica?

Is there life after death? And far more to the point, is there death after life? It is said that science progresses with giant steps. Given the rather modest shoe size of our race, can we realistically expect to keep pace? And then, what's the good of science anyway? Will we someday be able to log on to the Internet and surf atop Miss Italy? Will we be able to make love on line? Or would that short out the system? (In choosing the verb *to short out* I am in no way making a personal reference to anyone's anatomy.)

The world we live in has seen dramatic changes, including the toppling of the Berlin Wall—historical determinism or just shoddy construction? History is accelerating, political blocs are breaking up, liberalism is gaining ground. What will the new geopolitical map look like? A Jackson Pollock painting? Margaret Thatcher in profile? Can one still refer to a new world order, considering the total disorder in my room? What economic challenges do future generations face? What is the latest set of rules in the democracy game, and how many players does it take to make a side?

And now for the million-dollar question: why did my two-year-old niece learn to say the name *McDonald's* before my own? Is this the final conquest of consumerism, the total breakup of the family unit? I'm no biologist but I can't subscribe to such theories. I believe we are witnessing nothing less than the evolution of a new species, the *Homo hamburgerus*. No, not another sexual subdivision but simply someone like you and me, hobbled with complexes, a social security number, and a libido that won't let us get to sleep at night. It is in no way my intent to undercut the work of the anthropologist. My point is simply this: from the ages of stone and bronze, we have come to the age of the hamburger.

Having to date consumed 332 Big Macs myself, I can vouch for the hamburger as the single most accomplished expression of post-modern society (by *post-modern* I refer of course to the period spanning between Liz Taylor's fourth divorce and the invasion of Kuwait.) The Homo hamburgerus hypothesis allows an intriguing reinterpretation of the world in which we live. Above all, it permits us to settle once and for all the issue of collectivism versus individualism, of centralization versus the dictates of the free market. The revisionist hamburger is far more than the sum of its classic parts—meat, tomato, onion, pickle, lettuce. It holds more truth about our age than all the reports of the World Bank put together. It and it alone represents the purest expression of the collective unconscious. (One might call in Carl Jung at this stage, but in view of the lateness of the hour, I wouldn't care to disturb him.)

Given the universal appeal of the hamburger today, it is clear that liberal pluralist and consumerist values have outlived the last gasp of economic determinism. Dire proclamations concerning the fall of America seem premature to say the least, unless the country should for some mysterious reason run out of ketchup. For now, market forces rule—the very same forces that transformed Rabat's Soviet Cultural Center into a McDonald's. We've traded the blood of revolution for ketchup. For Tolstoy, Dostoevsky, and Turgenev the globalized comrades of Rabat now read Big Mac, MacNuggets, and MacChicken.

Certain observers would interpret the standardizing influence of the hamburger as a form of latent socialism. After all, the president of the company and the blue-collar worker consume the same sandwich—the same slab of meat and the same leaf of lettuce all bathed in the same sauce. But while these two very distinct social animals may be eating the same *type* of sandwich (not the *same* sandwich as may have been understood from my earlier phrase. These are undoubtedly troubled times but let's not overdo it!), they are decidedly not sharing the same salary, as the amount of money each receives is based on the number of newspapers he manages to read during working hours.

To avoid misperceptions of this sort, it must be clarified that the hamburger is hardly a socializing medium. How could it be when it in fact does not favor fraternity? The hamburger is an agent of autonomy, of self-awareness. It is a sort of gastronomic Ego pressed between two pieces of bread with a slice of onion and tomato, such that Descartes' "I think therefore I am" might as well read "I think therefore I ham."

In initiating our era of prepackaged take-away food, the hamburger has granted the individual an extraordinary degree of freedom and mobility. One is released from the standard institutional venues for eating (the restaurant, the dining room, the cafeteria) and thus from the social constraints connected to them. Now you can eat whenever you like and wherever you are. You can eat on the go if you want. The hamburger has heralded a raft of technological revolutions in this respect, starting with the transistor radio, that ingenious invention that made the notion of "portable" music possible for the first time in history. The transistor was followed by other innovations that emulated the hamburger in offering the individual more mobility: the walkman, voicemail, the computer, the mobile phone, to mention a few. I have reached the conclusion that indigestion and other complaints inherent to the consumption of hamburgers are actually the necessary growing pains (growling pains?) of the technological age.

I have produced these reflections under the influence of two Big Macs. Like the image of the world they reflect, the problem with hamburgers is that they are not always easy to stomach. I must therefore take my leave of this text, compelled as I urgently feel to deposit my thoughts on the new world order elsewhere.

5

MISS LIBERTY

I'd been living in anticipation for more than twenty years. It all started the day my teacher handed me a snapshot of an Amazon holding a torch, bearing the caption: "Liberty Lighting the World." But this was the real thing—I was on the Ferry connecting Manhattan and the Statue of Liberty, gliding slowly, the pure, still sea unravelling like a vast blue turban.

Standing at the rear of the boat, I watched the city draw away, and recalled these words from Celine: "New York is a town on its feet. Our cities lie down by the rivers or the sea, stretching into the landscape, awaiting the traveller; but this one refuses to bend—it stands erect, straight and intimidating." As we pulled further from shore, the sky-scrapers stood tiptoe, peering over us with their glass eyes.

The drone of the engines occasionally retreated under an upsurge of voices, describing and commenting in several languages. Far from being a punishment of God, the mish-mash of tongues was soothing to my ears, and I counted myself fortunate to be on board this floating Babel. A flock of Japanese tourists suddenly swamped the back of the boat, just as suddenly assuming a statuesque rigidity, their faces hidden behind the Cyclopean eyes of their cameras.

A little further up the bridge, a woman drew nervously at her unlit cigarette. Long red hair covered her shoulders. She wore a black T-shirt branded with a giant X. One got a white-marble glimpse of leg whenever the wind lifted her long skirt. She held a young child by the hand. With his emerald eyes and abundant freckles, he seemed to have stepped straight out of Mark Twain's novel.

The woman focused on some imaginary point over the horizon. There was an undisguised sadness in her voice, and an air of something submissive, almost broken about her. The child's least sigh was enough to upset her, and she strove to gratify the most far-fetched of his whims. She brought to mind John Fowles, and the French Lieutenant, so I called her Sarah. I imagined her joys and justified her pain. She would be taking the child to see Miss Liberty for the first time, after a long and exhausting trial over his custody.

The old couple next to me had struck up an animated exchange. The man was begging his wife to believe him, to at least listen as he explained how a French sculptor named Bartholdi and a French politician had given birth to the Statue of Liberty—how another Frenchman, Gustave Eiffel, creator of the renowned Eiffel Tower in Paris, had been charged with strengthening the structure that it might withstand the buffeting of the wind—how the statue finally came to America in 1886, dismantled and packed in 270 separate crates, a gift from the people of France to the people of America. But the lady was not interested. The sceptical face she turned to her husband was mottled with the million flecks of light that filtered through her wide-brimmed straw hat. How, she insisted, could Liberty, America's most cherished symbol, have its origins with "a bunch of French Anarchists?" Tom, meanwhile, was pointing at the statue and asking his millionth question—this time, why was the big green lady holding a cone.

A rustling among the Japanese signalled our arrival. I disembarked last, reluctant to break away, as if leaving an unfinished dream. And there she was, standing guard on a massive granite plinth, impassive eye some 150 feet overhead, scanning the horizon. She'd been dolled-up for her hundredth birthday. The robe's copper sheathing was cleaned and polished. The head and right arm had been reinforced. The torch was completely new, wrapped in acres of shining gold leaf.

This was no topless French Liberty in her revolution-red cap, wielding a pike, and the torch of arson and upheaval. This was the dear liberty of my dreams, the one I'd kept stashed away in my schoolbag, the liberty whose clear light illuminated the world by day or night, summer or winter.

At last I'd found her!

Miss Liberty welcomed me with a marble gaze too recently lifted to risk a smile. All hesitancy vanished. I plunged into the statue's base, where I found an elevator waiting. Less than a minute later, I was at Liberty's feet, snuffling among the folds of her skirt.

The spiral stair leading to Liberty's head and windowed crown was extremely narrow. We were doomed to climb single file, fenced in all round by a metal rail. We bore this fate in silence, bound for the moment in Miss Liberty's iron bowels. To get to the Light, one needed to climb higher, and yet higher, ever higher.

Constipated within that vortex of steel, I was no longer master of myself or my movement. One robotic footstep followed another, all roped to the robot drift of my body. As I ascended, my footsteps seemed to merge, to grow louder. For a moment I was able to survey my cellmates, caught like me on that spiral treadmill, confiding their innermost secrets and grievances. I watched one blow a kiss to his girl, like a last request before the scaffold.

Finally, after more than an hour's wait, I reached the crown and stood at the windows overlooking the sea. Through an enormous bank of steel bars, I got a glimpse of daylight, before being pressed toward a second staircase. This one was far smoother than the first; I practically hurtled to the bottom.

I left the statue drained, and walked into an abrupt wall of light. At my back, after a long and rather arduous digestion, Miss Liberty was calmly discharging visitors one by one, like so much excrement.

6

TELE-BLUES

I was in the lowlands, in a deep blue funk. I'd completely lost the appetite for living. Each new day turned up like the same reheated leftover—I could hardly choke it down. The salt of my life had decidedly lost its savor. As I'd done before in similar situations, I turned to the recipe given me by an old friend: "Whenever you feel like turning off your existence, just turn on a TV to remind yourself how fully life deserves to be sampled and savored."

Without a second thought I switched on the set to the 542nd episode of something called, I think, "As the World Burns." I'd missed at least twenty episodes; nevertheless, Laura, the golden girl with the flowing blonde hair, had scarcely moved. She seemed to be waiting for me just as I'd left her in a white leather armchair. The same black dress hugged her thighs and accentuated her breasts, and she maintained her air of beaten dog, with good reason as it turned out. Her husband, Ryan, just back from a long trip, had surprised her in the arms of his best friend, Allan, who having been surprised himself just the night before to find a young stranger smothered in his wife Angela's generous bosom, had sworn in the name of the Father, Son, and even Holy Ghost to cheat on the cheating Angela with no less than her younger sister, who happened to be none other than Laura—the golden girl with the flowing blond hair seated in a white leather armchair, wearing a black dress that hugged her thighs and accentuated her breasts—and Allan was in the process of doing just that with all his heart and soul when Ryan, his best friend, following a brief commercial message, burst into the room swearing in the name of . . . and the Holy Ghost to get even by sleeping with Allan's wife Angela, before remembering (after a second commercial break) that he'd already slept with her on the 329th episode, if not the 328th.

Instead of waiting for the credits to roll past that woeful backdrop, I switched channels and got the CBS News. The menu of the day was copious. Like everyone else tuned in at the time, I was treated to a succulent special report as an entrée. The press had lately become obsessed with "The Jogger of Central Park," a white teenager of sixteen raped by a gang of black hoods and left for dead. CBS had won the exclusive rights to broadcast amateur footage videotaped at the scene of the crime. The film was of poor quality and lasted only a few seconds, but one could clearly make out three black silhouettes setting on the victim with an appalling ferocity. Then a close-up of a tattered, blood-stained jogging suit—a forearm bearing a cigarette burn—a swollen face and breast, a shattered nose, an ear torn completely away.

I'd hardly had time to digest these juicy images before we were treated to a fresh serving, every bit as exquisite—an Indian specialty this time, spiced to perfection. Before a crowd of four thousand people a pretty eighteen-year-old woman by the name of Roop Kanwar had thrown herself onto the funeral pyre of her husband. This was done in accordance with Hindu tradition said the commentator on the scene, so that Roop need not outlive the man she loved. Roop's bones were crackling away like tinder as her ashes mingled with those of her husband. I comforted myself with a phrase from Schopenhauer: "No doubt it is revolting that a widow should be burned with her husband's corpse, yet it is no less revolting to watch her and her lover squander his hard-earned money once he's gone."

After the *flambe* we were served a few in-house specialties: a fatality on the interstate, a letter bomb, the wreck of a cruise ship, a mass suicide. There was a range of exotic desserts to finish off: a bloody civil war on the other side of the world, an entire community wiped out by an earthquake, children ravaged by famine, all garnished with a cadaver here, a monstrous crime there.

At this point I switched the TV off, pleased to have followed my friend's recipe. Above all, I was pleased to be myself. Once I'd finally gone to bed, I fell asleep with a pinch of ash, a dash of blood, and a drop or two of tears in the eyes. And in my heart, a thousand heaping teaspoons of happiness.

7

NEW YORK
AND MORE

I hadn't had a bite all day. I went into the 7th Avenue McDonald's, one of 25,000 in the city, and ordered two Big Mac Specials. It felt good in there. The cold on the other side of the door seemed miles away. A restaurant employee was busy trying to dislodge a derelict, whose snoring competed with the Musak. Outside, the metro mouth was coughing up a fresh clutch of passengers.

I attacked the first burger, eyes fixed on the street, on the city where everything is more imposing, more impressive, higher, grander, and of course bigger, much bigger, infinitely bigger. Starting with the subway, with its 715 miles of track, 469 stations, 5,950 cars—far and away the biggest urban transport network in the country. I thought on the sheer extravagance of this place, the most-filmed city on earth—110 films and 314 TV movies in a single year.

New York claims the country's biggest museum, the Metropolitan. And Wall Street, the biggest financial district—Macy's "the world's largest department store"—The Strand Bookstore, with more than eight miles of shelves, the biggest used bookstore in the United States—Barnes & Nobles, the nation's biggest book chain, boasting 355 super-stores, and 672 ordinary outlets—and the Verrazano Bridge, its nearly mile-long span, and more than 2 mile overall length making it the world's longest suspension bridge. As I swallowed my meal, I went on trying to swallow New York. Twelve thousand yellow cabs, 50,000 unlicensed "gypsy cabs," 5,600 plus miles of street, 4,600 bars, 70,000 boutiques, 450 manicurists, 1,000 antique shops, 750 pet shops,

100,000 artists, 170 spoken languages, 100 plus religious persuasions, 2 million Jews (making New York the Jewish capital of the world), and more than 100 theaters and 100 movie houses, just in Manhattan. Fifty museums, 500 art galleries, and 21 million phone calls per day, all in Manhattan alone.

I started in on Big Mac II. My neighbor was scanning his *New York Times*, one of the 2 million copies printed that day, and one of the nation's 1,765 dailies. Across the street, meanwhile a teenager was dipping into a garbage bag, looking for cans worth 5 cents apiece.

And now the statistics pressed in on me harder, like the hand of fate. Two thousand tons a day of household waste, 750,000 addicts (half the number for the entire country), 30,000 diagnosed cases of AIDS (another first, ahead of the entire state of California). Two thousand five hundred murders a year, and 25,000 prisoners, making New York the biggest penitentiary center on earth.

My thoughts were interrupted by a sudden cramp. I tried loosening my belt, taking a deep breath—nothing worked. Before long I was doubled over in my seat, unable to move. I still don't know whether it was the meat or the statistics; but something was terribly wrong with my stomach. It was the biggest case of indigestion I had ever encountered.

8

AFTER THE BEEP

The answering machine and I first met in New York.

I'd decided to call Reggie from JFK to tell him the plane had got in OK. Reggie is a lawyer of Jamaican origins who I'd met in the little coastal village of Asilah during his first visit to Morocco. We hit it off straight away, probably thanks to a mutual passion for women and music.

I dialed the number I'd written so carefully on my hand during the flight over. The call was going through. It felt good to be getting in touch with Reggie again. There was an abrupt avalanche of violins on the other end, then a voice ordering me to leave a message "at the sound of the tone."

For the first time ever on a telephone I felt caught in a trap. There was no time to reflect. I was denied the right to pause or to make a mistake. I had to deliver my message in a single shot. The moment they were out of my mouth my words were no longer my own. They'd been confiscated by a band of magnetic tape and anyone who felt like it could find amusement in my halting delivery. In addition, there was a fear of saying too much, or not enough, or. . . . I hung up.

Since then I've made my peace with the answering machine. Put on the spot by the beep, I've learned to make the most of my moment, to control the speed of my voice, get straight to the point, be more concise, more focused.

The answering machine had become something of a cult object in New York by the time of my stay there, moving from a simple useful gadget to a full-fledged medium of expression. The most self-conscious or least communicative of individuals was induced to try a hand at oratory or comedy. The messages people composed for their machines were meant to inform of course, but often their main purpose was to amuse, hook an ear, intrigue, astonish—in short, to seduce. What more ideal conditions could a budding comedian ask for, what with a captive audience bound to listen to the end with no chance of interrupting. Everyone who places a message on an answering machine realizes they are making themselves vulnerable, exposing themselves to the critical judgment of others. Nonetheless, it is the very fear of being ridiculed that puts a sharp edge to their creativity.

I met Lynne for the first time in the Strand Bookstore. Discovering a mutual passion for books and literature, we decided to get together again soon. But I was asked to first give a call just to make sure she'd be back from a weekend in Connecticut with her family. I dialed her number to get a machine with a satanic voice delivering this taped message: "*Salman Rushdie here. I'm not in just now and have no intention of telling you my whereabouts. All the same, leave your fatwa after the tone.*"

We were in the midst of an election year with George Bush Senior running for a second term when I called Bruce to let him know I wouldn't be able to make it to an appointment. This time too I got a machine: "*That's right, you have reached the White House. Leave a message after the beep and I'll answer your call if I'm back for another term.*" Then a confidential voice added with a jab at Watergate: "*I promise not to erase the tape.*"

It had been several weeks already that Lori had had her first child, and I still hadn't called to congratulate her. When I did, the baby was screaming full blast from the answering machine, possibly coached by a mother proud that her offspring should be flaying our ears. Then suddenly the voice of Lori, coaxing and sweet: "*Please leave a message at the sound of the burp.*"

Never willing or able to comprehend how I could get by without an answering machine, Reggie had asked me a few days earlier: "When are you going to grow up and join the twentieth century?" My Arab pride and I had had about enough by that time, and we decided to break down and buy ourselves a machine. The next day as I was absorbed in deciphering the instruction manual my attention was suddenly drawn to the TV. The news was winding down with a set of astonishing statistics produced from city police records: a suicide or overdose every seven hours, two rapes and a murder every five hours, sixteen break-ins and sixteen assaults every hour, a hold-up every quarter hour, a robbery every three minutes, an emergency every second.

Some time later I registered the following message on my new toy: *"You have reached 316-8835. I am not in at the moment. Please leave a message after the tone. Assuming I've not been burgled, assaulted, harassed, kidnapped, tortured, or killed I will answer your call the moment I get back."*

9

THE WOLF AND
THE RING

I don't put much stock in numbers, especially not since the day I was supposed to meet Reggie in the Village at one of those restaurants on West 4th Street. I was late as usual, only this time Reggie couldn't wait. He'd already had lunch and was just getting ready to leave as I arrived. We scarcely had time to say hello. Just before stepping out, he slipped a piece of paper into the pocket of my jacket. It turned out to be his napkin, neatly folded, on which he'd written the name and address of a Latin American discotheque followed by a prescription: "HAVE FUN!"

A few weeks later, as I was rummaging around for something to buy a paper with I chanced on that same note in the same pocket of the same jacket. There was nothing going on that evening, so I decided to pay Reggie's nightclub a visit, if not to dance then at least to hear some music. But instead of going to 204 28th Street as Reggie had intended me to do, I went to 26th Street. Reggie might have decapitated the eight in his haste, or maybe I just wasn't reading it right, as I'd gotten myself onto an obscure little side street where it was hard to make out numbers.

It took me awhile but at last I came upon something that could pass for the entrance to a discotheque. I knocked loudly, three times as per the set of instructions stapled to the door. A long minute later a man peeped through the spy hole and proceeded to open the iron grill that was holding us apart. With a blackjack in his hand and a head and face overwhelmed in hair, he seemed to have stepped straight out of the Stone Age. From a height of well over six feet he inspected me head to toe, shrugged his shoulders, and motioned for me to enter.

I followed down a long and winding passage, walls lush with graffiti. An assortment of lewd art welcomed the visitor—a giant phallus ready for lift-off, a spread-eagled woman, her genitals embossed with a swastika, here and there a call to revolution charmingly summed up in three words: "Fuck the Power." And liberally scattered throughout the entire tableau the inscription: "Hell's Angels."

This leg of my voyage ended at a sort of subterranean grotto peopled by an alien race. I wavered a moment at the threshold, long enough for every eye to find me and long enough to confirm that I'd got the wrong address. I'd unwittingly stepped into a den of Hell's Angels, like a sheep among wolves.

I could have simply disappeared the way I'd come, but for some inexplicable reason I made my way towards the bar, where I managed to straddle a stool and order a Schweppes. The barman had never heard of it so I had to be content with a tall and costly glass of mineral water. There was a buck-naked woman tattooed to his chest. Perhaps he'd met her somewhere back in his youth. They'd made love till dawn and just when he was experiencing a degree of pleasure he'd never known before, she left him high and dry. To get even he'd decided to make a second skin of her. At the slightest movement, when he bent over to serve a client for instance, he put her through a series of obscene contortions. She was so attached to him by this time that there was no chance of her ever leaving again. She traveled with him. She shared his bed and bath. She'd share his coffin when he died.

"Hi Skull." A woman's voice drew me away from these reflections. Skull was seated next to me. His features harbored the worst contagions of urban violence. That angel-face combined a swashbuckling moustache with the eyes of a bloodthirsty bat. Like his companions Skull had straight hair falling over his shoulders, patched jeans, spike-studded belt, rumpled blouse, leather boots.

He periodically dipped his face into a mug of beer to emerge dripping with foam. Beer trickled through his lips and down his beard to the heightened pleasure of his companion, a runtish woman not much higher than the barstool, who lapped at Skull's neck with her pierced tongue.

From time to time Skull drew at a hand-rolled cigarette, forming smoke rings in his toothless mouth and tossing them at my face—a welcome of sorts in the language of his tribe. As the smoke signals diminished Skull suddenly grabbed my glass and extinguished his butt in three dollars worth of sparkling water. For a second I interpreted this as a provocation, but soon realized that he'd simply burned his fingers and there were no ashtrays on the counter. At this point I noticed the curious steel band around his thumb—a ring, with the head of a wolf, muzzle agape, fangs bared.

Skull's colleagues were collecting around me, one by one. Some brushed my face with their long manes, their biceps thicker than my upper leg. They all took a long look at me as well. I inspected my image in the immense mirror back of the bar. Casually I unbuttoned my shirt, rolled up the sleeves, threw out my chest, furrowed my brow, drew in my cheeks, and affected a stony front. I passed a hand over my short hair and regretted my last ten trips to the barber. Each clipping of hair, each particle of dust brushed from a shoe, each wrinkle meticulously smoothed from a shirt—I mourned their passage.

That's when the laughter broke out, from all sides. Even the wolf on Skull's thumb seemed to be in on the joke. I don't recall very clearly what happened next, beyond backing timidly away from that den of angels, somehow negotiating the door, and hitting the street full stride.

I'll never forget that night. Even now Skull's wolf lopes beside me, presides over my insomnia, steel eyes never flinching. And the moment I begin to doze off, he bounds from the ring, leaps to my bed, skids along the sheet, and sinks his fangs to the bottom of my belly.

10

BEAUTY AND
THE BREAST

Ten thirty, maybe eleven a.m. A little park on the southernmost tip of Manhattan. Hudson Bay lies beyond the gutted chain link, its waters even murkier than the sky. A pale sentinel stands against the horizon—the Statue of Liberty, standing guard more than a century, torch in hand.

A vagrant wearing a black plastic bag for a cap is inspecting the benches one by one, scavenging cigarette butts and scraps of food and bottles with beer left in the bottom. As he makes his rounds our eyes meet, he gives me a big open smile revealing a gap in the middle of a brown set of teeth.

I'd been sitting there scanning the morning paper, either a *Daily News* or a *Newsday*. In the entertainment section my eyes had fallen on this headline: "Babies under Tight Surveillance!!!" According to the author, California (contrary to popular opinion) was not the most liberal state in the union, far from it. There in the land of stardust and skateboards, surfers and every conceivable kind of pin-up, a majority of legislators was in the process of revoking a law that would allow breast feeding in public, leading the journalist to conclude: "Babies beware. Nursing has just been declared an act of indecent exposure." Thus, the intent of the legislators was no less than to put a stop to the debauchery of whatever little nippers were abandoning themselves to public acts of indecency.

My thoughts turned back to a crowded train just leaving Marrakech. The only woman in our compartment was crammed up against the window. Large brown eyes highlighted with kohl shone from the glass. In a single triumphant motion practiced to perfection she freed a swollen breast and pressed it to the lips of her drowsing child, proud to display her womanhood before the world. The most insolent, the most corrupt eyes there saw nothing beyond a mother and welcomed the sight of her breast, source of life, bearer of infinite possibilities.

The legislature's mandate clearly showed that it knew which breast it was after. In condemning the nursing breast it had neglected to veto its counterpart—the breast flourishing in the streets and on the walls, at public beaches, in topless bars, on cinema screens, and between the pages of magazines the legislators were prone to thumb in private.

This is the pleasing, voluptuous breast as well—the one that titillates, that fuels our fantasies, that holds us in its spell. Like a Hollywood star it knows how to sell and indeed it does. It is exhibited like a piece of art for its beauty, sensual appeal, form, substance, perspective, structure. Its tightened nipple is set in the imagination like a bud about to open. Its hills and valleys beckon the photographer to enter a landscape of the imagination. Its satin curves accompany those of the polished car that invites one's caresses, or the still more subtle curves of the perfume flask one frees from its cage and holds in the palm of one's hand like a bird.

The California legislature fully understood that by the end of a term of pregnancy this breast of desire turns into a genuine threat. It may double, even triple in size, its translucent skin revealing a blue network of congested veins. It has then become a rebel, a nonconformist constituting nothing less than a triumph of womanhood. The superior notions of men literally fall flat. California had nothing against the breast of Eros and enticement and movies and Madison Avenue. It was the milk-swollen mammary gland they declared illegal, the breast that slaps us in the face with an apparently intolerable truth—we are part of the animal kingdom.

A rush of wings draws me back to the moment. The vagrant and the pigeons are competing over some crusts of bread. I close my paper and take a look around. The Statue of Liberty cradles a nursing child to her ample breast with one arm. She is flying the bird with the other.

11

FEEL MY PAIN

I had just one dream as a kid—to appear on TV. And if it could happen to Taybi, it could happen to me. Of all the kids in the neighborhood, he was the most inept with feet and fists, rendering him useless at soccer or self-defense. Shy and withdrawn, forever afraid of dirtying his clothes or breaking his glasses, he never joined our games. Taybi was a classic loser long before the term came into vogue. Yet, he was the one chosen to appear in a children's TV show I had watched religiously all my young life.

Taybi appeared briefly in an interview, and managed to squeak out a few words under prodding from the host. In that second or two, Taybi's stock skyrocketed—the screen had done wonders for his reputation, which continued to soar once he'd returned to the neighborhood. For me he had become The Great Taybi, the TV star, who I envied and adored at the same time. I begged him again and again to go over that initial episode of his show-business career, having no idea at the time that some 25 years later, I myself would appear on television courtesy of ABC.

It started with an unexceptional little notice posted at the university: "The Les Brown Show needs you! Contact Bonnie." I carefully took down the number, and a phone call later had half realized my childhood dream—they'd given me a reservation number and set up an appointment for the coming week.

Friday, October 8, six o'clock in the evening. Standing outside a studio on the corner of 1st Avenue and 76th Street. A day free from the standard drizzle; the crowd on the sidewalk in high spirits; the African American lady in front of me boasting that she had never missed an episode of Les Brown, except for the day of her mother's funeral.

I'd patiently endured the cold for a half hour or so, when I was handed a contract to look over, and then sign. There in black and white, I learned that ABC reserved the right to any images of me taken that evening, in part or in full, for use on The Les Brown Show or any other broadcast, advertisement included, on ABC or any other network, foreign or domestic. Once filmed, my image would no longer be mine, but the property of a company that had the right to use me to sell anything from shampoo to shaving cream, (though they wouldn't profit much from my stubble-free face or balding head). Seduced by the prospect of seeing myself on TV, I signed the contract, and in so doing agreed not to pursue a lawsuit under any circumstances.

Seconds later, I was inside with Lisa, who'd decided I was what she'd been seeking for the studio audience—just the right dab of color to enhance the overall composition. After examining at length my tanned complexion, the baggy blue trousers, the white sweater, my trusty green-striped shirt, Lisa opted to put me in an aisle seat, next to a heavily made-up African American woman in her late forties or early fifties.

It was at this point that Bonnie—the same Bonnie I'd spoken to on the phone—made her appearance on the set. The mental image I'd composed from her voice was a far cry form the androgynous reality, and I felt somewhat let down. She was wanting to know if we were ready to welcome the one, the only, the incomparable Les Brown, and if there was anyone in the audience who had come out of their way to be on the show.

"New Jersey," someone proposed tentatively from the back.

"Florida!" another called boldly, as if he'd come from the ends of the earth.

Raising a sage-like finger and wearing a triumphant smile, I pronounced three clear syllables: "Mo-roc-co." The word drew an instantaneous and universal "Wow!" making me feel like some great trans-Atlantic explorer.

Now Bonnie was wanting to know if we felt we could compete with the show's prior audiences. If we wanted to be up to snuff, it was vital that we follow her instructions closely. She began by entreating all those devotees of nose-picking to abandon their hobby during the show. We were asked to defuse the beepers on our watches, to relieve bladders or bowels according to need, to get rid of our gum if we hadn't already done so, to control our emotions, smiles and tears, to abstain from scratching backs or scalps or noses or chins or ears, or any of the other options. We were like those stroke victims who have to be taught all over again how to breathe, walk, smile, exist.

Our re-education lasted a little more than a half hour. At last we were ready to live the long-anticipated moment. Was it really happening? Bonnie asked that we do one more trial run through a round of applause, the very heart and soul of a talk show. The trick was learning to clap together, with the same air of conviction, the same eloquence, the same intensity.

As this was a critical maneuver, we were turned over to Lara, an applause specialist. Some are born to lead, some to instruct, some to govern—Lara was born to clap. It was her field, and not as undemanding a field as one might first believe. It required a certain flair. I tried to picture Lara at home, the consummate professional, practicing each morning, beginning with some simple hand to hand, then picking up the beat—harder, faster, harder and faster still. The maid overhears, sticks her head in, not for the first time, and says: "You called, madam?" Lara doesn't miss a beat. Her tone is chilly: "Why is it so hard to get good help? Can't you see I'm working?"

It only took Lara a few minutes to turn us into masters in the craft of applause. We clapped on cue, with just the right dash of passion and verve. Then Les Brown appeared, to general acclaim. He was an African American in his early forties possessing the requisite elegance and charm, expression, and slightly mocking smile. Les gave us a quick overview of the day's fare, just enough to wet our lips. The show would last ninety minutes. The theme was "Family Reconciliation." There would be eight commercial breaks. For now Les asked us to welcome Jack, the first guest on the show, which we harmoniously did under the baton of our maestro, Lara. Jack was a good-looking, well-dressed African American man of thirty years. With perfect poise, he recounted the history of his homosexuality. Since childhood, when he'd been raped by his uncle, Jack had fled the world of women, and flown to the company of men. Apart from his sister, Dionne, no one in his family had been able to forgive his sexual preference, least of all when they'd learned he'd contracted AIDS. It occurred to me that there was little gay about being gay, at least not in this case.

Les Brown zeroed in on the relationship between Jack and his older brother, Al. It transpired that Jack had not seen his brother for more than three years—more precisely, not since the day Al and his wife, Sandy, had come to visit him in the hospital, on which occasion Jack had accused his sister-in-law of taking advantage of his weakened state to steal $400 from the bedside stand.

At that moment, we were stunned to see Al himself walk onto the set, and privileged to witness firsthand this unrehearsed family reconciliation. After years apart, Jack and Al were together again. All was for the best in this best of all possible studio worlds. Arm in arm, the brothers fell into tears, which soon gave way to sobs, which in turn gave way to the first commercial break.

During the pause, generous hands issued the more sensitive among us with tissues—the rest were offered caramels or chocolate. The show was put on hold a few minutes while Les Brown took a powder. He then came back to joke with the audience. On the air he'd been wearing a sad face, and seemed rather choked-up by the family dramatics. Once the camera stopped rolling, however, he turned his back on the guests and dedicated himself to amusing us with his jokes, all of which ended in gales of laughter.

As we came back on the air, the accomplished Les Brown instantaneously reassumed an air of beaten puppy to introduce the next guest, a psychologist. Seated between the two reconciled brothers, she explained with extravagant gestures and frequent allusions to Freud, how the source of their estrangement was not the accusation of theft, but Al's refusal to come to terms with his brother's sexual orientation. We were formally prompted to acknowledge this startling revelation with a round of applause. The analyst had, predictably, opened some old wounds, and the brothers were soon overtaken by another ardent and obviously cathartic shower of tears. More adds, more Kleenex, more sweets, and more jokes against the backdrop of family affliction. Thus we commuted between laughter and tears and back again, until the shooting wound to a close, and we were finally instructed to leave the studio in deference to security regulations.

Friday, October 22, ten o'clock a.m., the magical moment. The world around me had paled—my eyes were on the TV. The various segments of the show unfurled with no great surprises. Les Brown was in top form, appearing both moved and moving. I searched for myself in vain. There was the guy from New Jersey, there the one from Florida. For a split second, I thought I spotted the colorful garb of the lady seated next to me.

The Les Brown Show was drawing to a close, and I was losing hope. Abruptly, the screen yielded a white sweater, and a green-striped shirt . . . and there it was, obviously proud to be on the show, my imbecile face gaping straight into the camera.

12

CAPPUCCINO

I remember it vividly. Like every Saturday afternoon, I was on the terrace of the café where I liked to sit over a cup of cappuccino, basking in the movement of girls along Broadway. It was my pleasure to collect, at a glance, a complexion, gait, smile, mood, lock of hair. Before me was a world of beauty filled with creatures whose bodies—be they ample or frail, be they sculpted within a severely utilitarian dress, a pleated skirt, or something far more revealing—it was my duty to flesh out.

Dazzled in the flow of form and color, I often forgot my own presence at the café, becoming merely an eye open to the street. Sometimes I liked to select one of these women at random and intrude a bit further—give her a name, age, place of birth, invent for her a childhood and a destiny, imagine for her a lover waiting to steal a last kiss before the departure of a regrettably punctual train.

That particular day my eyes had fallen on a woman who seemed thoroughly absorbed in the rhythms of the city. Then abruptly, just as she passed my table, her pace slackened. She turned her head, looked at me, and gave me a smile before being carried away by the crowd. From the moment I saw her I was sentenced to love her futilely. The next two weeks saw me in the same café every afternoon at the same table. As I'd done that day, I ordered cappuccino and pancakes with maple syrup. My determination was such that I even insisted on being served by the same stylishly ungroomed waiter, as if reconstructing the scene to the least detail might draw the lovely woman back to me. During my remaining months in New York, however, I was never to see her again.

Despite the time and distance that today separate us, I retain the vision of that woman just as it appeared one summer afternoon, and would like to attempt a portrait, in an effort to make her immortal. I choose my material—a sheet of lead, mute, opaque, carefully polished to a reflection of her skin. I take my chisel and endeavor to render forever the face that will not leave me. My wrist feels the resistance as the tool furrows deeper looking for a black as intense as her hair, her eyes, that glance. Now the hand lightens up, freeing the tool to scratch rather than bite, trying vainly to give form to the memory of a face. The outline, the form, the proportions all look right. What I am unable to catch is the depth of those eyes watching you without really seeing you—eyes that hold the look that started the Odyssey.

I put up the chisel, grab a brush, dip it in memory. Deftly my hand executes a portrait of a woman. She is perfect and bears a striking resemblance to my model, but the flash of that glance, the texture of that skin, the smoothness of that hair, the firmness of those lips, the blessing of that smile . . . all these are missing. The internal half of her glance—the voyage without end, a geography of the soul—eludes my brush.

It's no good. I give it up. I turn off the lamp and light a candle, reminding myself that one sees most truly in the dark. And it's a fact. There in the wavering flame I find her complete. The softness, the whiteness of her skin—the warmth of her body and her eyes . . . they are there, yet flickering just out of reach, on the verge of disappearing.

Drawn forward, I approach the light softly, cup it in my palms. For fear it may go out I hold my breath.

13

NOUS YORK

Nous York Sidi, with its 1001 minarets, is a city like no other. The Grand Mosque of the World Trade Center, its twin spires rising more than 400 meters, calls the faithful to prayer in ever-increasing numbers. Like a giant index finger raised to the sky, the Empire State Building evokes the oneness of Allah.

The Friday prayer over, open carriages line the long walls of the city or clip-clop towards the date palm groves of Central Park. There, under a symphony of birdsong and fountain the families on board will savor *bastila* (a light crusty pastry stuffed with chicken and almonds), the inevitable seven-vegetable *cous-cous*, and a lamb and prune *tajine* left to simmer all day over a clay brazier. Elsewhere among the city's innumerable rose and jasmine scented gardens, lovers seek the shaded refuge of an orange tree to speak with their eyes the language of the heart.

Sombreroed water bearers roam the subway stations jingling their bells, pouring cool water perfumed with juniper oil from their goat-skin bags. A makeshift orchestra on one of the platforms improvises a *melhoun* of lutes and tambourines. Up in Rockefeller Plaza people are discussing sports scores in animated gestures, while a troupe of *gnaoua* musicians dances itself into an epileptic frenzy under the din of drums and brass castanets.

A thicket of luminous signs tells the time in Time Square along with the temperature, weather forecast, and breaking news. Immense billboards vaunt the benefits of ever-better, ever-newer products. A human mosaic decorates the plaza under the gaze of a giant brunette. There are acrobats, jugglers, quack doctors, snake charmers, ape trainers, and a horde of tourists desperate to experience the "exotic." Here is someone touting a miracle potion against ill luck, there is a fortune teller reading palms, and a bit further on the storyteller's drum and shimmering voice lure passersby in quest of dream and illusion.

Night falls, the crowd thickens, spills about the improvised stands that offer mountains of tangerines and boiled eggs, or the traditional clay bowls of *harira*, skewers of grilled meat, sausages spiced with paprika, doughnuts deep-fried on the spot.

On Broadway not far off Time Square, theater lovers flock to see Laalej's new play, and yet another production of a classic by Saddiki. Further up the intricately tiled sidewalks a large group of journalists attends the premiere of the new Tazi showing at the Warner Cineplex.

Radio Sidi Music Hall is sold-out this evening despite its 6,000 seats. A crowd of music lovers, tickets in hand, is about to sit devoutly through an evening of Andalusian music under the direction of Rais, the maestro. Nearby, Madison Square Garden is anticipating a much larger crowd to welcome the return of the cult group *Nass Al Ghiwan*, after several years off the scene.

Further east, Ghallah is signing copies of his 21st book at the Barnes & Noble on 5th Avenue. The reviews in the *Nous York Times* are calling *The Buried Present* a "book of great maturity and depth."

Lying along the edge of the date palm grove the country's largest museum, The Metropolitan, with its distinctive green-tiled roofs and whitewashed walls, is staging a Cherkaoui retrospective after the stunning success of its Matisse in Morocco exhibition.

Sifting through these memories, I feel like I am back in the days of the glorious Moroccan Colonial Empire, when New York City was still called Nous York Sidi—when the city's symbol was a glass of mint tea, not an apple.

But what do you want? One can't change the course of history.

14

FRUIT COCKTAIL

I really didn't feel like going out that Saturday. It had been a lousy week, and I was all for going to bed early. The telephone determined otherwise—it was Reggie, as usual, proposing I accompany him to a party, where, he said, I would experience the very underbelly of American society.

Reggie's sense of humour was only surpassed by his fondness for women, and I felt compelled to take up his invitation. The sluggish mood was gone. We arranged to meet shortly at Canal Jeans, a well-known Soho boutique where we often made our rendezvous. On arrival, I learned we had been invited by one Diana, Hawaii-born, who was celebrating her birthday as, indeed, she always had done since moving to New York at the age of sixteen. All we had to do was find a Hawaiian shirt to wear. For the price of a new shirt, I was able to scrape up a faded blue second-hand model adorned with pink blooms. I wore it half-buttoned, not from any wish to expose my hairless chest, rather for the simple fact that there were several buttons missing.

Twilight found Reggie and I outside an unassuming building on the West Side. The whole area was dark, save for an apartment three floors up, where light filtered through the blinds. At the door we were met by the smiling Diana—a slightly built woman with honey-coloured eyes. She was naked to the waist. The number twenty-five was painted on her breast, one digit per gland, the way the more conventional would have had it frosted on a cake. Before I could introduce myself, Diana embraced me as if we were old friends. The tobacco-alcohol stink of her breath would hound me the rest of the night.

From the look I shot him, Reggie understood that he owed me an explanation. He had just forgotten to mention certain details, foremost of which, that we'd been asked to a boobs party, to a festival of breasts, all bare save for their owner's choice of garnish.

I hesitated. The room was huge and hot. Moreover it was festooned with joyous, provocative, brightly decorated bodies. A fleshy woman lay on the floor, clad only in army boots. A pair of pacifiers dangled from her swollen breasts. A band of young Hispanics whipped out salsa music. A couple slow-danced, suspended in their private, steamy universe. Guests mobbed the bar, where I spotted a Levi's tag pasted to an admirable rump, in turn pasted to a stool. A space goddess perched on the window ledge, breasts housed in a pair of aluminium funnels held in place by a metal wire round her neck. The firm, black, lustrous breasts of the woman beside her were adorned with a pair of enormous seashells.

Someone's voice, Reggie's, brought me back to earth. "I'd like you to meet Lori," he was saying, in a deliberately sensual tone. Tall and slender and young, Lori probed me with her eyes, incited me with her smile. Slowly, with an infinitude of little reluctances, she proffered her cheek, as if afraid she might drop something. My gaze instinctively plunged into hers, then dove a bit lower to the impressive breastworks mounted on her torso, suspended within the half-shells of a split co-conut. While I listened to Lori talk, I took in the clusters of cherries dangling from her ears, the sliced pineapple bracelets made of fluores-cent rubber, the wild strawberry wedged in her navel. A splendid fruit cocktail! An appetiser to take the breath away! "All that's missing," I mused, "is the banana."

I averted my gaze a moment to pursue the latest arrival—a beauti-ful brunette with azure eyes. She moved languorously, thumbs hooked into a pair of jeans that fit her like a second skin. Her bare breasts were painted with giant replicas of her own eyes—for pupils, a set of brown nipples, with two blue areolae making the irises. Those eyes stared at me without so much as a blink. "Big Sister," I thought, "is watching you."

I forgot everything and everybody—the music, the dancing, Reggie, Diana, Lori. . . . The party had vanished, the room was empty, there was only her standing before me. I made my advance, skipping the intro-ductions, and murmured: "You really have a lovely pair of eyes."

15

A DOG'S LIFE

On my way through Hartford, Connecticut, I couldn't resist a visit to the Samuel Clemens estate. Clemens, better known as Mark Twain, was at once a pundit, storyteller, humorist, and author of *Tom Sawyer* and *Huckleberry Finn*, works that helped assure his rank as one of the greatest American writers of the nineteenth century.

After spending a pleasant, and rather moving, afternoon at the Twain mansion, I chanced upon a boutique for dogs, a regular canine paradise crowned with an elaborate sign. "LICK YOUR CHOPS" was its name in giant neon.

Several customers browsed the food section, where in addition to the usual tinned or dry food, you could choose from a whole range of sweets and treats. There were big chocolate cakes for gourmand dogs, delicate honey cakes for gourmet dogs, and salt-free biscuits for the health-conscious dog.

For a few paltry dollars you could commission a T-shirt, a scarf, or a tie bearing your dog's picture. Be it poodle, Pekinese, or merely mutt, a likeness was available on calendars, wallpaper, paintings, miniatures, murals (9 by 12 feet), wood, bronze, or ceramic sculpture, mosaic, and even tapestry.

Nor has "LICK YOUR CHOPS" neglected your dog's personal wardrobe. Elvis buffs can dress their hound dogs in black leather jackets embossed with an image of The King. Rap connoisseurs can dress theirs in fashionable motley, with caps to match. More lavish customers can have a fur coat tailored to measure, and a fur hat to go with it, or choose from among the racks of silk evening dresses glistening with rhinestones.

Fear not—death itself need not separate you from your dog. "LICK YOUR CHOPS" can help you prepare for the world to come. If you are Christian, why not make your dog one too? And celebrate his salvation with a specially priced velvet dog cassock, decorated with an ornate cross in the colour of your choice. If you are a Jewish, consider a yarmulke for your dog, or offer him a handsome outfit stamped with a Star of David.

I left "LICK YOUR CHOPS," and was headed in the direction of my hotel, when I stopped dead in my tracks. A newspaper had wrapped itself around my ankle. The headline read: "150,000 Somalians to Die of Hunger before Year's End."

16

IN THE ORIGINAL
IF YOU PLEASE

As far as I know the New York cinephile is the only biped that would sooner be led to the butcher than see a dubbed or even subtitled film. Leo Tchestopol, prominent critic and cofounder of the review *Arrete ton Cinéma*, sums this attitude up perfectly when he writes: "In an authentic Italian film even the dogs bark in Italian, and it little matters whether they do it with a Roman or Neapolitan accent."

New York has a number of theaters catering to true believers who must have their films in the original, without subtitles. One of these, the least known I suspect, is located between the headquarters of the prestigious Association of Vegan Philosophers and a little fast food outlet regarded by many New Yorkers as the Mecca of the cheeseburger. It was into this movie house that I happened to duck out of a downpour one afternoon in a desperate bid for shelter. A square tilted slightly to the right, a horseshoe topped with a crescent moon, a bowl in blossom, and a circumflex being struck by a rod was the title of the Japanese film they were showing (the reader must forgive any spelling mistakes). The title suggested some light comedy, three or four dirty bits, and a little action. I parked my rear in a plush cushioned seat and awaited the credits.

A procession of giant flyspecks began scrolling up the screen, maintaining the same steady pace. I say "giant fly specks" though it was hard to be sure from such a distance. They could just as easily have been the tracks of a huge marine organism with the head and body of an ostrich, the ears of an IRS auditor, and the finely carved feet on a piece of Louis

XV furniture made of precious wood. What I was seeing might even be, though it was impossible to really know, the footprints of the immense quadruped whose perfectly preserved skeleton had miraculously been discovered standing upright in the main hall at the Museum of Natural History. According to the excellent and informative handbook, *The Illuminated Cavern*, this creature was capable of making a sound approximating the voice of Pavarotti on a mobile telephone, although since the museum's opening it had kept perfect silence. As the author points out, one needs to consider that the unfortunate beast spoke no English, let alone English with a New York accent.

As for me, I understand not a single word of Japanese, and need to acknowledge at this point that the opening scenes of the film presented certain difficulties. There was a haggard-looking man kneeling low to the ground, wearing slippers and speaking to a tree. He gestured broadly, now with his arms, now with his nostrils. The tree was in its early thirties, some sort of briar or elder (unless it was one of those hall trees they sell at Ikea for $10 a piece) that had already lost all its leaves. It took no part in the dialogue and made no gesture, content to hold forth its trunk as if to say: "I may be only a tree but I wouldn't mind someone's scratching my back."

From the intensity of the man's rhythm and phrasing, the situation seemed to be getting serious. I scrutinized his face, watched his every move, listened intently to his voice. Most likely he believed in reincarnation. He was possibly in the middle of a conversation with his own grandmother, asking her to bless him and wrap him tightly in her branches. The man spoke and spoke, on and on. What about? I was hardly in a position to guess. But why should it matter? I don't know what the flowers say to each other either, yet can't help being overwhelmed when someone hands me half a dozen.

In the next scene the man joined a woman seated at the foot of a bed. Before saying a word, they bowed to each other barely escaping a concussion each (I am perpetually amazed that such rituals do not require one to wear a helmet). After that the man started to get very worked up, asking curt questions and speaking injuriously to the woman. I say "injuriously" because from the way he showed his teeth (fillings, crowns, bridges, the works), it was fairly evident he wasn't pitching woo. From time to time, in his rage, he spit in her face, thus pronouncing her maiden name. But what do you want? Not everyone can be called Abu l'Harith al-Zamakhshari.

Hanging her head, the woman answered in short phrases similar to the cheeping of a sparrow. This is not an allusion to her movements—only to say her voice sounded like the chirping of a sparrow, or like the sparrows that chirp back home, at any rate. A second later the man's eyes had filled with tears, the woman was choked with sobs, and both were exchanging fragments of speech that completely escaped me. Apparently the man had something against this woman, as he had begun shaking her roughly like a common can of shaving cream or a bottle of pop. The reader will likely object that these are hardly the same thing. All the same, it looked like it hurt.

I was trying my best to follow the scene without actually meddling in their affairs, but certain questions kept coming back to me, marching single file through my head in chronological order. Just what did that man have against the woman anyway? Had she let some dark secret out of the bag? Had she forgotten to pay the electricity bill? Had she been the bearer of unwelcome news—the death of a friend perhaps? A parent? His beloved grandmother? Had someone cut her down in cold blood just so they could warm up? Or maybe the woman had betrayed the man. As she and her lover fled, passion overwhelmed them in the car. They ran a series of red lights, parked in a clearly posted No Parking zone, and surrendered themselves to the urgencies of the flesh on the back seat. That must have been it. The man felt humiliated. Could he ever forgive the woman for violating his code of honor? Or worse, for having so flagrantly violated the traffic code?

At present the man, looking haggard and kneeling low to the ground, wearing slippers and speaking to a tree, was gesturing broadly, now with his arms, now with his ears. I experienced an eerie feeling of deja-vu, and used the opportunity to treat myself to a brief intermission. I slipped off my shoes, unbuttoned my collar, loosened my belt, and took provisional refuge in a nap. I say "provisional" because no sooner had I closed my eyes than the couple re-emerged in period dress. Disguised now as Lady Macbeth, the woman was shouting that all the water in the sea would not be enough to wash the smell of sushi from her hands.

I woke to find the man brandishing a sword above his head. Had I missed something? Admittedly, he had a tough-looking beard and prominent chin but the size of that blade seemed excessive. He sank slowly to his knees as if to pray, then with surgical skill performed a magnificent abdominal incision (known as Harry Carrey among baseball connoisseurs), liberating the entire contents of his veins down to the last corpuscle. Just before the end, he looked at the woman through dimming eyes, as if to say: "Goodbye for now, it's only temporary. You'll be climbing my trunk and picking my fruit soon enough."

After the final credits (I'll spare any details concerning flies and other monstrosities), I put my shoes back on, buttoned my shirt, tightened my belt, and stepped into a pelting rain. As I was thinking things over later in the snugness of my bed, I still wasn't sure whether I'd seen a comedy, thriller, or love story. But what did it matter? I had seen the original version.

17

RUBBER SOUL

That I actually managed to pronounce the word in public must be considered a miracle in the history of Bleecker Street. The pharmacist had already been a long moment peering at me over his spectacles. He was dressed entirely in white. His hair was tied up under a beret, a few locks straying down to his eyes. He was simultaneously chewing gum, tapping his foot, and humming a rap version of *My Way*.

"Condoms?" I ventured at the third attempt, pulling it off in a precious-sounding English worthy of the Duchess of Kent. He turned mechanically to the cupboards behind and stepped up on a stool. His fingers ran along the shelves like a librarian's until at last they paused and flipped a number of boxes into a basket, which was then placed under my nose. I watched owlishly and kept my mouth shut. There were enough condoms on the counter to outfit an entire regiment of Marines.

"With or without the reservoir tip?" he inquired, readjusting his spectacles. I rested my elbows on the counter, puffed out a cheek, dilated a nostril, and tilted my head ever so slightly toward the door. Loosely translated into the Queen's English, this meant: "If my liege will kindly forgive me, I haven't the slightest intention of running the Indy 500 or the Paris-Dakar. A few short excursions perhaps, which I categorically refuse to make in a convertible considering the sort of filth these streets have been known to fling up."

"You need to consider," he said, with a little tug at the beret, "that before selecting a tire it is essential to know whether you'll be taking a back road or not." He then launched into a penetrating dissertation on the human anatomy, unrivaled in depth save perhaps by Jules Verne's *20,000 Leagues beneath the Sea.*

He removed the glasses and reflectively bit one of the bows. "Perhaps you have a preference for a particular style of driving? A tendency, shall we say?"

I blinked vigorously and tilted my head first to one side, then the other, as if to say: "I have spent most of my life on the left with a slight leaning to the right, and since the fall of the Berlin Wall, on the right with a slight leaning to the left. I have been known to use the right blinker when turning left, and (though far less frequently) the left when turning right. That is probably why when left alone in a room with an eighteen year old nymph, I hardly know which way to turn."

He handed me a stiff blue cardboard box, then some advice, using the same slow patient tones one employs with a child: "If you're the cautious type, better have a look at these—the Durex Doublex 008, contour fit, fluorescent (in case you care to scout ahead) with double-thick reinforced walls to ease the worst anxieties. Security-wise, I can hardly recommend them enough. From the sensitivity angle though, your lady will confirm that she'd sooner ride with Sir Lancelot in full armor."

He then seized a small red box and held it to his nose. "Hot Rubber Sweet," he announced, taking a deep sniff. "This one's strawberry flavored. We also have them in mint, chocolate and vanilla. Just in case you'd like a little appetizer before diving into the main course."

He paused, gave a slight nod, and continued: "Or you might prefer, in boxes of twenty, these "Khondomz Magnum" designed for larger dimensions. I might as well tell you straight away though, they do tend to slip off if you're not actually packing the meat."

The fingers fished back into the basket and came up with a black box, which he held under my eyes. "If you'd like a change of look you might consider the opaque "Dark Rubber." He shifted his weight to the counter and spoke confidentially. "Not everybody's got a pink weenie you know."

I slowly closed my eyes, moistened my lips, and gave four sharp raps on the countertop. Translation: "It's been more than fourteen centuries now that my ancestors left Arabia to settle in Africa. They were never in the habit, to the best of my knowledge, of applying a hypoallergenic total screen with vitamin E and UVA/UVB/IR protection. In other words, my friend, I've had ample time to get a tan."

"For really long-lasting protection I strongly recommend this one." Now he was handing me a flask hardly larger than my thumb. I inspected it closely, holding it in the hollow of my hand as if to determine its weight.

"Read the directions carefully before application, otherwise you risk losing a lot of skin those first few days. You can't be too careful, you know. Lots of things can upset it—heat and cold for sure, but also sun, wind, dust, and above all pollution. You should also avoid washing it with strong detergents."

I looked at him, hitched up my brows, and rolled my eyes clockwise, signifying to anyone with eyes to see: "I am not in the habit of sunbathing nude next door to a nuclear reactor, nor is it my intention, now or ever, to run myself through the wash cycle, however much I may need the exercise."

I'd spent about twenty minutes in his company, but in spite of the world's best intentions was still unable to make up my mind. I sighed deeply and gave him a blank look that meant: "I'll need some time to think this over." And with the perfect seriousness of a child at play, I went off to savor the pleasures of abstinence.

18

BLACK AS SNOW

In New York City, Snow-white is black.

One summer day, a woman sat down on the curb, and stuck a needle into her weary veins. Three drops of blood fell to the street. The crimson seemed so lovely against the glistening asphalt that she said: "If only I could have a daughter black as this street!" Soon after, the wish was fulfilled. The woman gave birth to a little girl black as asphalt, who, for some unknown reason, was called Snow-white. Shortly after the delivery Snow-white's mother died of an overdose.

Her father, who squatted precariously in a flat in the South Bronx, was soon to take his leave as well. Consumed with sorrow, with no place to live, he eventually shot himself in the head. So it was, that at the ripe old age of nine, Snow-white walked alone into the jungle, where dealers, skinheads, cop-killers, and other wild animals lurked.

Months turned into years, and Snow-white into an attractive young woman, who one day stepped into a sex club on 8th Avenue called Seventh Heaven. Every night since, she'd stripped to the seamy inspection of the crowd, and like the girl whose story she'd once been read, waited for her prince to come.

More months passed, and more years; still, Snow-white waited. And when at last she could wait no longer, she went into her room, fired up a joint and, perched atop a cloud, she said to herself: "Men are only dwarves, after all."

19

PARADISE LOST

In retrospect, I never should have picked up the phone. I was sitting at my desk reading, when the call came. The woman on the other end was asking, with no preliminaries, if I'd ever been to paradise. My first thought was that this must be one of Reggie's little jokes, but then I remembered he'd just left for Jamaica. As I had still said nothing, the voice again demanded to know if I really had never been to paradise. The papers at the time were full of the phone killer—a maniac who got his jollies strangling people with a telephone receiver. My tongue was tied. For a second, I saw my name on a bloody list of victims. It seemed that for whatever unknown reason, someone was volunteering to expedite my eternal journey. "I'm sorry," I murmured at last. "You've got the wrong number."

But no, there was no mistake. The suave, slightly sinful voice belonged to a woman doing telephone promotion work, who was merely wondering if I'd been to Paradise, the New York club with the pleasantly infernal reputation. The incomparable Paradise, where every man dreamed of going some day. For ten wretched little dollars, drink included, I was being offered the chance to discover fifty of the most beautiful creatures on earth, all eager to make my acquaintance. The voice on the phone became hot and sensual, breathing out an address, phone number, and finally a big sonorous kiss that would have given a hard-on to a corpse.

I hung up, the burning in my ears spreading slowly to the rest of my body. Before long, I'd been not only ignited, but altogether consumed. It took forty-five minutes to reach the threshold of Paradise, where two rather grim guardian angels had posted themselves like sphinxes. Uncertain what to do, I handed each a ten dollar bill, just happy to be able to cross into the Promised Land at last. Inside I was asked, to my surprise, for a third ten-dollar bill, which I relinquished to the persuasive blond behind the counter. For only five dollars more, she assured me, I could make use of the cloakroom. These people were certainly thoughtful. With the assistance of an adorable little creature who wouldn't stop undressing me with her eyes, I managed to get rid of my coat, scarf, gloves, and five scraps of paper bearing the likeness of George Washington. "After all," I consoled myself "It's best to go in empty-handed."

A hostess appeared from nowhere and begged me to follow her. Clad in nothing apart from a filmy strip of fabric passing as a dress, she slouched lazily away, seeming to take pleasure in mocking me with her chubby cheeks. I followed through a maze of flesh. Here and there one spied a stray article of dress, a revealing cut of cloth, a roaming breast, a barely veiled inner thigh. Frigid-featured wax dolls came and went in every direction. They came alive at our passage as if under some enchantment, setting up a palpitating, trembling abandonment to desire. Each one held me momentarily in a tender gaze, with eyes that read: "For Hire."

The hostess at last deposited me beside a graying man dressed in a three-piece suit, attended by a pair of plump angels who were powerless to take their eyes off him. My hostess continued to hover, once I'd taken a seat. I slipped her a liberating bill, and she vanished.

At the same moment, two feverish lips attached themselves to my ear, and I felt a hand at my thigh. A voice, scented with alcohol and cigarette, declared its indignation at finding me by myself, and offered to keep me company during the show. I was moved by this gesture, and readily agreed to share my table with anyone willing to pledge her alliance for an entire evening. She was surprised to learn I came from Africa, which she considered the loveliest continent on earth, and even more so to hear I was from Morocco, the loveliest country in the world, the very place she'd always dreamed of spending her remaining days,

She snapped her fingers loudly, summoning a large black attendant, who appeared before us wearing nothing but a grin. When I mentioned that I didn't drink, my companion ordered me a glass of juice, with a gin twist for herself. Babe, if I remember her name correctly, was extremely tactful. In the course of the evening, she agreeably accompanied each $5 glass of juice I ordered, with another $15 gin twist.

Against a disco background, a voice announced the arrival of China, a lovely brunette with oriental eyes. The way she passed her tongue over her lips certainly got a rise out of the man in the three-piece suit. Abruptly, China tossed her head, releasing a cascade of hair. She began to massage her breasts with her long fingers, then her entire body, without neglecting a single curve or cranny. Commentary and nervous laughter were soon springing up from all sides. Babe asked if I was enjoying the show. I nodded my head, and otherwise ignored her.

For that moment, naked under the arc lights, China was intent on shinnying up the steel shaft mounted at center stage. Once at the top, she slid slowly back down, straddling the giant member between her legs. Soon the demonstration had reached a point of such conviction that Presidents Washington, Lincoln, and even Hamilton were bowing at China's feet. I put in my share when the time came.

China left the stage, trampling the carpet of dollars, and made straight for my neighbor, who welcomed her with his loud laugh. She'd doubtlessly read something profitable in his gaze. Without warning, she seized his tie in her hand like a limp member she was intent on reviving. My neighbor seemed to appreciate her efforts, for the more she tugged at that piece of silk fabric, the more he tugged at his wallet. Although China was obviously not interested in giving my tie a workout, she reminded me that it was really my duty to give her a little something, if only as a show of solidarity to my friend.

Grace Jones, meanwhile, had begun belting out her rendition of *La Vie en Rose*, as background for the arrival of the inimitable Rosy. Rosy was a rose indeed, losing her petals one by one, right down to the lace panties that eventually fell to her feet. This time, it was my turn to enjoy a more or less private taste of paradise. Planting her elbows firmly on my table, Rosy proposed to pick up a greenback using only her breasts. The perspective was so interesting, and the execution so conclusive, that I parted with a second, and then a third bill.

After Rosy, came Bambi, Clara, Nina, and the rest. In the space of two hours, I saw more curves, breasts, and bottoms than I had seen in all my life. I left a last tip for the attendant who accompanied me to the door. Then, my mind flush with images of bare flesh, and my pocket bare to the last penny, I stepped out of Paradise into a pelting rain.

INTERNET
CHEWING GUM

A cud-chewing cow is a contented cow—there's no room for doubt.

Since getting to New York I have taken up gum-chewing, which I guess is in some ways better than crack cocaine. Everyone here chews gum from the lowliest dealer down the street to the President of the United States. The hip-rippling prostitutes on 42nd Street chew gum. They do the chewing; passersby do the salivating. The big executives on Madison Avenue chew it, as do Reggie, Jenny, my neighbor across the hall, and even my goddess vaulting about the dance floor with the grace of a leaf carried on the wind.

Chewing gum is to America what the French fry is to Belgium, tea to Britain, wine to the French, and couscous to the Moroccan—it is a national cause. To ignore it is to fail one's duty. To abstain is treason. And so one chews and when one can't any more, one goes right on chewing. Of course it is necessary to eat something now and again, if only to keep mom and dad and Aunt Betty and older brother happy. Despondently, you remove your wad, roll it between index finger and thumb, and throw it away. There is some consolation in the thought that cleaning your teeth no longer depends on that gum-flaying, tongue-rasping, palate-scouring plastic brush. According to the dentist, a fresh stick of gum is all you really need. And in case your jaws are exhausted the eyes can take over. TV is there to take care of you, filling those long evenings at the touch of a button with images for the mind to chew on. Rest assured, you need never run short of provisions.

No, chewing gum will not rot your teeth. That's Communist rot, they're holding a grudge. No, chewing gum will not give you wrinkles—more back-biting Communist propaganda. Listen to Wrigley instead. Wrigley? Surely you know him, the patron saint of chewing gum, the Rockefeller of cud. According to Wrigley his product aids digestion. Back in 1915 he was the first to position chewing gum next to the cash register in restaurants, the first to send gum to children on their second birthday—not (God forbid) from any wish to secure their dependency but merely to wish them well. In addition, chewing gum helps one concentrate, work harder, produce more. Wrigley is clear on this—gum is the best friend a working man ever had, especially in times of crisis or need. Marx had it all wrong—better for him to have invested his thought (and money) in chewing gum.

Exercise your thyroid muscles, brothers and sisters! Champ, chew, masticate, munch! The white, the pink, the yellow! Strawberry, licorice, banana! Those with comics, those with riddles, those without riddles! Chewing gum, brothers and sisters—there is nothing more. It's a form of behavior, it's oral masturbation in the words of my analyst, it's an endless folding back upon itself—in sum, a philosophy, whence the motto: "Me first, me next, me always." And if by chance you should try to distance yourself from this reality (by blowing bubbles, for example) the whole thing is likely to go off in your face.

One could plot a road 5 million miles long with the gum chewed each year in the United States alone. This is the stuff of dreams and visions. Bothers and Sisters, rejoice! You are not alone. Others have followed that straight and narrow path. The French now spend 1.9 million francs annually on gum; since 1962 the Japanese have promoted an association called *Let's All Chew More Gum*. And it goes without saying—the French and Japanese have class!

Brothers and Sisters, I have a dream. I see Black and White chewing side by side. I see the sun coming over the horizon and the brilliant glistening sea. I have a dream where men, women, children, and old people chew hand in hand. Brothers and Sisters, there is a new day coming when we will be linked together, when our separate roads will converge at last. A day is coming when we will all chew as one! More than the conquest of space, more than the battle against racism, hunger, or AIDS—the chewing-gum superhighway is the real challenge before us. Together we can go far, to Mars if we want, and make the Martians green with envy. Who knows? Perhaps we will reach the sun itself.

Chewers of the world, unite!

21

FLIGHTS OF FANCY

I've always had a weakness for the Italians and I've always been drawn to the world of fashion. Still today, despite an onset of baldness, chronic stomach ailments, and abrupt hot flashes every first of November during leap years, I feel a thrill to witness a procession of pretty girls. In other words, I was very pleased the day providence slipped a formal invitation through my mail drop.

It was the wrong mail drop, as they'd written the address wrong; nevertheless, they were requesting the honor of my presence at the Givenchy premiere of its spring-summer collection. At the bottom of the card someone (who I imagined to be an extremely charming someone) had added in red ink: "Don't forget your tie. Cheers, Paula."

I had never myself had an occasion to wear a tie but felt reasonably sure the word referred to the strip of fabric people knot about their necks, preferably beneath a collar, and whose sole function is to restrict the flow of air to the lungs. Admittedly, there are exceptional cases of advanced pathological regression such as those described by the eminent Wolfgang Bermsgaden in his *Theoretical Treatise of Applied Psychology* (Vol. 3) in which, for reasons still unknown to science, the tie may at times serve as a bib and vice versa.

In any event I borrowed a florid tie and a three-piece suit to go with it, and presented my invitation the following Saturday at the doors of a fashionable Madison Avenue boutique. Paula proved a pleasant receptionist though she obviously thought I was someone I wasn't. After seating me next to an urbane lady of sixty-odd years (who could easily have been taken for Elizabeth II if not for that silver crown on her lower right molar), Paula asked if I'd had any news from Angela. I knew of no Angelas but said she was doing well. "In fact," I added optimistically: "Wonderfully well."

Paula had an angel's smile and a walk capable of making the blind to see and the lame to tap-dance. I immediately ascertained that she was not a Marxist simply from the way she rolled her hips. A second later as she leaned over to pick up the invitation I'd dropped, I was able to confirm that she voted Republican. She was, it must be noted, not just any sort of Republican but the right sort—the kind with long legs and curves to make a cello pout.

In short, Paula was gracious and lovely. Owing to a skin-tight flesh-toned gown, from the distance she appeared to be entirely nude as well, an illusion belied by the tight strap barring her bosom. This seemed to me a crime against nature. Paula had no more right to bare her breasts than my *concierge* back home had a right to bare her legs. To look upon Paula was to tremble in awe at the handiwork of God Almighty. Such perfection, such charm! For the first time in my life I found myself resenting the fact that the ways of the Lord are impenetrable.

Yet again, I didn't know whether to talk about Abu Zayd al Quraishi, the urban kif-smoking scene, the effect of power outages on the de-mographic curve, or simply to slip her my card (that part of the male anatomy designed to spare us the burdens of conversation urged me towards the latter option). Having thus successfully postponed a mean-ingful discussion, I had a glance at my program.

A half hour later Paula's velvety voice was presenting the new Givenchy collection. One by one, five birds of paradise which M.A.L.E. (Mothers Against Lame Eroticism) will not permit me to describe in detail, paraded their plumage to a techno beat.

My neighbor to the left, a journalist from *Cosmopolitan*, spent the entire time explaining to his neighbor (not me, the one to his left) the ideological significance of this spring-summer collection in light of cer-tain geo-strategic developments in the wake of the Gulf War.

Thus, the mini-dress with the strapless bodice fastening at the back and embroidered in white lily of the valley on gossamer; and the stretch crepe georgette corseted gown buttoning along one side and zipping along the other; not to mention the sensible little jacket in hand-dyed silk, "Claudine" collar, and three-quarters navy sleeves; and finally the red organdy lace gown trimmed in delicate mother-of-pearl buttons with wide sleeves pleated in at the shoulder, a sailor collar, and white taffeta fretwork throughout offset by a pair of ornate flowers in silk braid. . . . All expressed a profound ethnic-religious malaise. All pointed to a decadent West nervously watching the rise to power of certain emerging economies and fundamentalist movements.

I'd seen one of the models go by in a white silk evening gown that I thought of giving to my girlfriend back in Morocco. On conferring with Reggie the next day, I was assured that the plan was not entirely beyond my means but that it would first be necessary to have my gold crown pulled and sold, the remaining days of my life pawned against a roll of ready cash, and finally to be patient for several thousand years until my skull had had time to bleach in the sun and could be excavated and sold for a pretty price at Christie's.

The show closed with a superb wedding dress. We were then all invited to cocktails on the house. I didn't think twice (or even once) before accepting, eager as I was to rub shoulders with the city's movers and shakers.

The first person I encountered was one of those habitués of Wall Street. He talked like a financier but certainly didn't look like one. I could more easily picture him doing a tap dance routine or serving drinks in one of the gay bars on 8th Avenue. His moustache was so thin it might have been penciled on.

He acknowledged my presence and forged ahead: "The Exchange has certainly been bullish these past few weeks. Even so, it was hardly a surprise when G.T. fell through, was it?" Then, calling on me to witness, he said: "Of course, with a P.E.R. of twenty-four, what did one expect?"

By way of reply I nodded slightly, scratched my left ear, and arched my eyebrows severely, which carried several possible interpretations: "It's the same with chimpanzees and all the other primates"; "Life is certainly full of surprises"; or alternately, "Yesterme, Yerteryou, Yesterthey."

"The way things stand now," he continued, "chances of that Brown Group merger falling through seem out of the question. They and their associates have got 43.7 percent of the shares already—it's only a matter of time till they get a majority."

He took a fresh look at me and added in paternal tones: "Of course, that all depends on whether Johnson, Woods, & Levert are prepared to stay the course. Michael Woods' decision to leave could certainly throw a wrench in the works."

I had a few thoughts of my own on this matter. I wanted to observe that God is great and Mohammed is his Prophet, that if G.T. was going down it was assuredly because at least one of the above wanted it that way. For a moment I even considered telling him what had happened to one of my old college friends. We'd just cashed our checks and he was relieving his bladder under the sober gaze of a local candidate posted on the wall, when an enterprising thief took the opportunity to steal his stock. I wasn't convinced my story was worth telling, however; and besides, someone behind us had started talking about painting, my favorite subject. I decided to abandon G.T. to destiny.

I approached the artist reverently. At the first opportunity, I anxiously pursed my brow and cut into the conversation: "Would you care to comment on the current decline in the Arts?"

He raised an eyebrow and regarded me curiously as if to say: "I wasn't aware the Martians had landed."

"Decline? What decline? You have before you a man who to date has sold (he consulted a black notebook the size of a matchbox) 413 watercolors, 522 drawings in pencil and another 373 in ink, 854 oils including 65 diptychs and 36 triptychs, and 23,030 silk screens not to mention more calendar and postcard reproductions than I'd care to count.

It might interest you to know how I got where I am today. It wasn't easy getting started. I'd pick up a few pennies here and there doing abstract designs in chalk on the sidewalk—barely enough to plug the hole in my belly. And then one day a dove landed close to where I was doing Mondrian's *Broadway Boogie-Woogie*. It makes me ashamed to admit it, but my first thought was of having the thing served up in a bag of Kentucky Fried Chicken with duck sauce and ketchup. But in a moment of inspiration I drove back my hunger and drew the dove on the pavement. Before very long I'd drawn a crowd. They thought they'd discovered a rare bird in me, apparently. From that day on I've painted nothing but pigeons, and the stool pigeons just keep flocking in. I've got five years of backorders, people are snatching up my work all over the world. I guess a bird makes the perfect painting—it's pretty, it's pleasant, it's simple. Best of all, it won't shit on your sofa.

I continued to listen as he described how from a miserable struggling artist he'd spread his wings and gone on to become the greatest poulterer in the city. For some reason his story was making me hungry. We shook hands warmly, and I headed for the buffet.

That's where I met "Holly" engulfing a huge slice of pizza and half a dozen lemon tarts. He'd taken his name in reference to Hollywood. Holly was hairy as a bear though completely bald up top. He looked like an immense ball of grease wrapped in a red blazer, but inside that greaseball was hidden a vast knowledge of film, about twelve volumes' worth. Even as a child Holly had a hard time fitting into an armchair, and had maintained tight links with the cinema ever since. He was a diligent presence on the set, at openings, at film festivals, and had for long commanded the obituary page of *E.T.* (*Entertainment Today*), a bimonthly dedicated to the world of show business.

He knew everybody in Hollywood from the head of Warner Brothers to the cleaning lady. In less than fifteen minutes it was my privilege to discover the brand of Al Pacino's favorite boxer shorts, Sharon Stone's bust size, Robert Redford's steadily growing interest in the sexual life of penguins, Brando's struggle with premature ejaculation, the name of Clint Eastwood's mother-in-law's gynecologist's wife, and not least, the alcohol content of Michelle Pfeiffer's deodorant. Ignorance of this last detail had till then constituted a glaring lacuna in my knowledge of the cinema.

In the space of a few minutes all my most venerated stars lost their shine, and in less time than it takes for my neighbor to fall for a TV actor I was smitten with an ugly case of cinephobia.

Since that night I've not finished a film. I've tried, but the second the projector lights go on I grab my seat and start screaming. I can no longer tolerate people's talk on the subject. At the mere mention of the word "cinema" my entire body breaks out in hives with the exceptions of my left calf and my chin. The monosyllable "film" is enough to coat the bottom of my tongue with cankerous sores, once causing me to say "Nice twat" instead of "Nice thought" at an unfortunate charity dinner, and occasioning two of the loudest slaps witnessed in the postwar era.

Back in Morocco I went through a stream of dermatologists and torrent of village marabous before crash-landing at last on a psychiatrist's couch. Eighteen months of analysis later I was made consciously aware of my rare diagnosis (exceedingly rare in my country)—"cinematography complex"—and was prescribed a brand of eye drops called Film-Away. Though I continue to flee the movies, I've got rid of the bothersome fuzz-balls that used to drift across my field of vision.

Upon learning the size of Woody Allen's right shoe I abandoned Holly to join a group of gentlemen discussing the environment. They seemed deeply concerned about the future of planet earth. I still recall how I astonished them with a brilliant expose concerning the impact of minarets on the ozone layer, supporting my argument with the work of an Israeli environmentalist whose name (though very like that of a Lebanese pastry) eludes me now.

A small, impeccably styled man in his fifties put a hand on my shoulder. His hair was plastered back, and he wore a three-piece suit.

"And you?" he inquired. "What do you do?"

I said nothing, my eyes staring at a pair of flies performing their version of the Ode to Joy on his shoulder. I would have liked nothing better at the time than for him to have been abruptly smitten with amnesia, or equally adequate perhaps, for the Empire State Building to have fallen on his head.

"And you?" he said again. "What's your line? What are you in at the moment?"

Once again I remained silent. I had my reasons. I wanted to say that at the moment I was in a profound state of embarrassment, or to be more precise, that I was in really deep shit, and that in any event I didn't feel like talking without my lawyer present.

Just then a waiter came by supporting a silver tray on which sat a cake wearing a string of pearls and mounted on a slab of vanilla ice cream coated in dark chocolate. From the look of things, I'd just been saved by a confection. I said: "I'm in the food industry."

The charmer from Wall Street was back. Instead of another of his meditations on how fluctuations in the stock market influence the sexual behavior of the American middle class, he now wanted to know if I was into cereals. My experience with cereals at the time was limited to corn flakes and whole-wheat toast. Not knowing quite how to respond, I tilted my head slightly to the right, then to the left, as if to say: "You're warm, but not quite."

"Fish perhaps?" he said.

This time I had to acknowledge that he had sniffed me out, that I was indeed into fish. I spoke impulsively and regretted it directly.

I'd never set foot on a boat in my life. Just putting my feet in the tub was enough to get me violently seasick. I knew about fishing what my grandmother knew about Einstein's theory of relativity, what Shakespeare knew about the Internet, what his Holiness the Pope knew about late developments in Afghan pornography. I didn't know the difference between a shrimp and a swordfish—which ignorance had once earned me a spine in the throat and consequently last place in the singing contest after dinner.

There were, I admit freely, some glaring deficiencies in my piscatory prowess. I am today able to recognize a can of tuna at the supermarket but for many years I thought a whale was some sort of pneumatic device. For many years my secret wish was to prick one with a needle to see it transformed before my eyes into a flying sardine. By the time I'd read *Moby Dick* I still couldn't understand how Captain Ahab could have risked life and crew to get even with an air mattress.

Which brings us back to that evening and that delightful group of men determined to suck the marrow from the specialist in their midst. The oldest of the group seemed particularly pleased to meet me. From boyhood on he'd developed his passion for canneries, fish canneries in particular. He was curious to know the distinction between deep-freezing and mere freezing, between smoking and kippering, between a pickled herring and a potted haddock, and whether there was any truth to the claim in the latest issue of Fish News that *Mrs. Paul's* fish sticks contained traces of fish.

He'd hardly finished when the man to his right broke in: "It is hardly my place to speak to someone of your stature concerning the development of a death-wish within the fish population following publication of *The Old Man and the Sea*. Nevertheless, is the rumor one so often hears true that suicidal tendencies have lately been observed, particularly among red snappers that feel blue?"

I looked at them both in silence. I was having a very difficult time coming to a decision. Should I massage their backs with a monkey wrench or serve them their teeth in a popcorn bag? I eventually said that according to the available evidence the only significant difference between freezing and deep-freezing was in the prefix, that smoking and kippering were interchangeable, that herrings and haddocks were currently out of season, and that a suicidal tendency had indeed been verified among fish sticks, not among the red snappers as previously held.

With a brisk nod my dearest friend resumed the reins of the conversation. "Allow me," he said, "to draw on your expertise with just one more question. As a long-time practitioner myself of surf casting, trawling, and (though far less frequently) spear fishing, I suspect that you yourself would favor a purse seine over a gill net, drift net, set net, or even a fish trap. But notwithstanding one's taste in nets, when using bait is it better in your opinion to go with eggs, spoons, spinners, lures, squid, chum, or the ever-popular worm on a hook? I'm sure I speak for everyone here when I ask—to what do you attribute your success?"

This time my inclination was to clean his teeth with the monkey wrench prior to massaging his back.

"Various experts in the field," I replied, "have looked into the matter and their findings are conclusive. Some fish are consummate gourmets, some are vegetarian, others follow strict low sodium diets, a few observe kosher, a few, like the *piscis capillus fanaticus*, won't even look at pork. Asking me to say straight off what bait is most suitable is rather like asking someone to say what the lady at the next table is going to order as an entrée."

I was up and running now and nothing was going to stop me. "To be successful in fish one must at times sail through troubled water, into the teeth of the storm if necessary. It is essential to keep one's bow to the wind and one's hand on the tiller, to take in sail if need be. One must at times rise to the bait, but with caution. At times it may be advisable to toss out a red herring, to stand between the devil and the deep blue sea; even, God forbid, to go down with the ship. But this above all else—to have read *Robinson Crusoe* at least once in an unabridged, pleasantly illustrated edition."

I spoke then on the importance of fish in the work of Kierkegaard, in the writings of Cauwelaert (particularly in his second novel *Love Fish*), in the Egyptian underground cinema, and in the recipe "Sole with Sorrel for Four" (preparation time: 25 min.; baking time: 40 min.).

By then it was evident that I'd gained their respect, but it was getting late. I took my leave on the pretext that it was still a forty-five-minute walk to my place on the East Side, upon which my Wall Street friend proposed to see me there in his limousine.

"That's very kind," I said, "but I prefer to walk. You know how it is. When you've been to sea as long as I have, you never pass up an opportunity to feel dry land under your feet."

22

POOR ME

I made her acquaintance one evening at the home of H. Rosenberg, eminent member of New York's International House, and first-rate tango dancer. She was a pale, sickly woman with blank eyes set in thick lids that seemed to be bearing the grief of the world.

"So, you're from Morocco," she said, between nibbles of caviar and smoked salmon. "It must be tough being from a country where there's nothing to eat."

Not knowing quite how to respond, I merely reminded her of the suffering apparent from the South Bronx to North Harlem. The gutted shops, the burned-out buildings, the innumerable ill-lit, cold-water tenements crammed with whole populations consumed by hunger, fear, and hopelessness; the countless panhandlers and homeless people one saw each day criss-crossing the street, or pursuing their "careers" in the subway system; the children huddled together for warmth in the carcasses of abandoned cars, too weak and weary for play.

Unfazed, the lady was running her eyes over the magnificent spread. When I'd had my say, she turned her cold fish gaze on me and murmured in my ear, like someone betraying a secret: "Get this straight, young man. There are no poor people in this city, just deadbeats."

There it was, then. I'd forgotten we were in a democracy where one could choose to be poor or rich, sick or in a good health. Between smoked salmon and hunger, between sable coats and bitter cold, between luxury and poverty, the poor had cast their vote.

It seemed that Henry Miller was right after all, when he said: "If shit is ever worth anything, the poor will be born without assholes."

23

MASC./FEM.

I've never been sure about the sex of the angels. On the other hand, I know how to tell that of the nations. My very first grammar lessons revealed that the world was divided in two—the masculine and the feminine. No place name was exempt from the rule, which was enough to convince me of the superiority of my native land. For me, there was absolutely nothing in common between Morocco (le Maroc, masc.), virile and splendidly mustachioed in my mind's eye, and the neighbors (l'Algerie, fem./la Mauritanie, fem./la Libye, fem./la Tunisie, fem.), who all wore skirts. Learning that we were a kingdom (un royaume, masc.) and not a republic (une republique, fem.), I expressed my subsequent notions of dominance in an ink drawing on my school desk, far too lengthy to allow a reproduction here.

Many years have gone by since then and I'm in New York, thousands of miles from home. Nevertheless, I am obsessed here on the 110th floor of the World Trade Center with the need to lift this city's tail and discover what it is.

Having visited before, I know how cold New York can seem to the visitor, but its frigidity is only on the surface. You may penetrate cautiously or go in full of apprehension, but you will always come away dazed, disoriented, tormented, changed. New York is a fascinating town, at once seductive and deeply demanding. The Big Apple has to be bitten into, at the risk of leaving behind your teeth. A few steps in and you're caught up in the commotion and ceaseless come and go of the crowd. It's like being in the arms of a faithless woman. You're aware of deception, of danger even, but you can't do without her.

Not everyone shares the same attraction to this city, however. At the end of his first visit to New York, Nikita Khrushchev, head of the Supreme Soviet in those days, declared to the press: "I don't like the life here. There's no green anywhere. A stone would get depressed in this place."

This statement leaves a distinct aftertaste of the Cold War. Then too, if Khrushchev felt so stonily dismal in New York, might it not have had something to do with the constitution of his heart? Otherwise, how do you miss the dozens of admirably designed parks? New York is flecked with a total of 840 acres of trees, gardens, and stretches of water. Central Park serves as the city's purgatory—a place to let off steam, reach a climax, suffer, rejoice, even bleed. One always leaves the park breathless.

From the top of my tower I look out over the city a last time. Manhattan is furrowed with streets like stretch marks on a body that has grown too fast or grown weary of childbirth. Far in the distance, Central Park is a dusky tuft of shadow, perfectly proportioned, receptive, open to my desire.

I hold out my arms and cry aloud: "New York is a woman!"

A girl with her nose in a guidebook offers the hint of a smile. I see her again at the bottom a short time later. Our eyes meet. I say on impulse: "What's your opinion? Is this city male or female?"

Her eyes turn back to slide up 450 yards of glass, steel, and concrete. In a voice that clearly believes itself to be stating the obvious she says:

"Looks male to me!"

24

SAINT TECHNO

One afternoon as I was strolling through Greenwich Village I stepped into Tower Records to look for a hard-to-find album I'd been after for ages. There in the jazz aisle I caught sight of a beautiful woman of Slavic origins, whose boldly painted lips were offset by a large pair of sparkling eyes. She wore a yellow beret and had an album in her hand—the same album I'd been so desperately seeking, and I thought: "We may have completely different backgrounds and physically we're miles apart, but at least we share the same music." The relationship initiated by our subsequent conversation lasted all winter, till the day she reckoned her prince had come in the form of a London-based Palestinian journalist.

At age fourteen, Jenny, whose real name was Natasha, had emigrated from Moscow to San Francisco with her engineer parents. When I met her she was in New York doing a PhD in physics at Columbia.

Inviting her out proved easy. As Jenny eventually confided between bites of lasagna, there was a Jewish something about me that she found irresistibly attractive. By our second date she had started calling me Joseph and all efforts to get her to use my true name were simply viewed as the tantrums of an Arab with an identity problem. She refused to allow that any name save Joseph could adequately convey the fullness of my lips, the smoothness of my cheeks, the brightness of my eyes. In vain I explained to her that I was descended from the Prophet Mohamed (Peace be upon Him), even offering to have a copy of my family tree sent over to prove it, at which Jenny made a face that made me think of the monkeys in the Jemaa El Fnaa Square of Marrakech.

Perhaps this was simply her way of saying we all had a common ancestor somewhere.

These details are simply to provide a backdrop for the winter evening when I discovered a place I will never get out of my head. On one of our first times out, once we had established a mutual interest in dancing, Jenny asked if I'd ever been to a Chelsea club called The Limelight. I said I hadn't but was pleased to display my familiarity with a long list of nightspots from the S.O.B. to Danceteria and points in between including the Xenon and the Copacabana. Jenny did not seem particularly impressed. "Well you haven't seen anything yet," she said in a voice that had something of a balalaika.

The very next day we were among the pilgrims, some from as far away as New Jersey, flocked expectantly in the open air. I was still looking around for The Limelight when Jenny pointed it out—the Church of the Holy Communion, built in the nineteenth century and bought in the 1980s by the diabolically visionary entrepreneur, Peter Gatien, who'd had the place rechristened and converted to suit the disciples of the night. For legions of hopheads and cokeheads and just plain young people out for a good time, The Limelight was a window on paradise, quite literally so, as you had to be chosen to get in.

We'd been in the cold for more than an hour anticipating a sign from the guardian angels posted at the gate, and at last one motioned us forward. His providential gesture signified nothing less than our salvation, and we surged forward to join the elect of God.

Once inside, Jenny and I were no longer able to communicate save with our eyes. The music was ear splitting, the crowd invasive. The mahogany bookcases, pulpits, and communion tables of the barely transformed church were still in place, serving heavenly cocktails to the faithful. Further in, the vestries that had once held holy relics were now boudoirs holding clouds of smoke, where makeshift liaisons materialized at the mercy of the music. Other pilgrims made their appointments among the pews or prie-dieus, vainly trying to communicate in the thunderous din. Strobe lights and lasers flickered from the nave, not candle glow. The cross behind the altar was turned into a giant screen where video images flashed at dizzying speed under the crucified gaze of the devoted.

The DJ stood suspended on high in a priest's frock, substituting the bedeviled rhythms of techno for the weighty chords of the pipe organ, to the intense satisfaction of an enthralled congregation.

I tried to catch someone's eye, or smile, but the faithful were sunk too deeply in their meditations, seemingly tuned to a world I had no access to. I felt a sudden mix of loneliness, there in the midst of the multitude, and of revulsion. I wanted to cry out against this sacrilege like a voice in the wilderness; I wanted to hurl my indignation into the faces of the damned, this profane mob. Just then Jenny caught my hand and I managed to read her lips:

"Well, what do you think?"

"This is Hell," I said impulsively.

"What?"

"HELL!" I roared.

"I knew you'd like it," Jenny said.

25

MISS MAMBO,
HAMLET, AND ME

In his "In Praise of Slowness" Albert Memmi tells the following anecdote:

"A woman was in the habit of saying things like, 'I'm going to put together a quick meal so we can have a quick lunch, and that way we'll have time to catch a quick nap.' To which her husband added: 'And that way we'll have time for a quick death.'"

Isn't it the truth! I myself am a believer in slowness. Like the woman's husband, I feel that the attempt to move through life quickly serves to lead us all the more quickly to death. For me, slowness is a way of life, a way to get back at time. It is nothing short of a vocation. Of course there are heaps of other things I know how to do. I can talk with my mouth full, spot a worm shining on a plate of spaghetti, and make my teeth chatter whenever danger comes around. But being slow is the thing I do better than anything else in the world.

I've often been asked how I manage to look so young. You may not believe it, but I have never used any creams or rejuvenating products of any kind, neither am I on a special diet. My secret? Slowness.

Old Albert would agree that slowness is a form of spiritual mastery leading to the mastery of one's own body. I have cultivated slowness from the very beginning, such that today, under instruction from my spirit, my body is living in slow motion. People in a hurry, on the other hand, are going at such a frenetic pace that even the most microscopic cells in their bodies rattle uncontrollably. It's hardly surprising to find these people growing wrinkles on their wrinkles in less time than it takes to write about.

Believe me, slowness is the only reality worth the trouble. The problem in New York is that it's not possible to eat cheaply unless you go to a fast food place, even though eating at McDonald's, or Burger King, or Subway amounts to sacrilege for someone like me. You've got to get in line fast, order fast, chew fast, swallow fast, digest fast, and. . . . It's best I break off this sentence fast in deference to those of you reading this at the table.

"You know what?" I asked Reggie one day. "I've about had it to here with fast food. You always feel like you're eating under the gun in these places. I hardly have time to sit down before someone's dropping hints that it's time to clear out."

"I know a place in New York," he replied, "where you won't find a single New Yorker. The service is slow and there's no chance of feeling rushed. Just be sure you take something to read."

I took down the restaurant's name and address and stopped by Barnes & Noble that very evening to pick out a book. Hesitating over *How to Invest in the South without Opening your Mouth*, a current bestseller on how to be heard without saying a word, the *Rubaiyat* of Omar Khayyam, or something by Shakespeare, I wound up buying a paperback copy of *Hamlet*. A little later *Hamlet* and I were walking into Reggie's restaurant. I chose a table by the window and plunged at once into my book.

Hamlet, for those who've not read it, is the story of a crown prince who suspects his uncle of having murdered his father in order to seize power and squeeze Hamlet's mother the Queen. In the first part of the book Hamlet is torn between murder and suicide—in the last part, between suicide and murder. It's a matter of self-respect really, and of course hatred. By play's end the stage supports a generous mound of corpses, Hamlet's fairly near the top. I do not mean to be facetious here, for death is hardly a laughing matter. The dead are aware of this firsthand—you rarely find them joking around.

A waitress showed up at my table thirty minutes into the book. She had the loveliest smile on the East Coast—a smile to melt half a dozen banana splits along with whoever had ordered them. But we're jumping ahead—it's not time for dessert yet. She was beautiful and tall and she wore a pair of tight red shorts that served to make her the center of attention for every man in the room. At the slightest movement, part of her anatomy commenced dancing the Mambo—which part in particular

I am not inclined to broadcast to the entire world. I will only say that without it, we would find ourselves swaying like old rocking chairs each time we sat down.

At this point objections may occur among sensitive readers. As for the others, it is my assumption that theirs have already been raised (the reader will guess that I refer here exclusively to virile males in good health). I am aware that many female readers are on the verge of tearing out this page to fold themselves a little paper boat. As far as these are concerned, the remarks I've made with regard to the Miss Mambo are proof enough that I am the sort of man who left the cave a very short while ago, if at all. I could not agree with you more heartily, dear ladies. Like you, I believe men have not changed a whisker since Neanderthal times, though they've learned to shave them off on occasion for job interviews.

Returning to our topic, Miss Mambo was there waiting at nose level, and something about the way she held her thighs convinced me she was not an enthusiast of Nietzsche (or if she was, she hid it well). What she hid less effectively was the double airbag, an optional extra of silicon wedged into black velvet upholstery and thrust so close it succeeded in tickling me in precisely the spot a woman's curves are supposed to tickle. I know, I know. . . . You're going to say the airbag metaphor is not a happy one but in similar moments of crisis, who among us could claim to be happy?

Her name being nowhere on the menu, I inquired after the special of the day.

"Fish *consomme* and chili con carne," she replied in that delicious way of hers.

"Chili con carne?" I thought this was some sort of joke at first and later confirmed it once I'd lifted the first spoonful to my lips—it was a joke, and in bad taste too.

But once more we are jumping ahead. I was not to see the Miss Mambo again until I'd already finished the first three acts of the play. Just as I was ready to dig into the fourth she served me a bowl of steaming water in one smooth motion. I stared at it a long time trying to decide. Like you, dear readers, I knew the anecdote about the man who mistook a finger bowl for beef tea and drained it to the last drop. With the grace of a pianist I did what you would have done in my place—I dipped my fingers in the fish consomme. But such is life, and tragedy for tragedy, I allow that Hamlet's was more distressing.

I dipped back into my book, finished it, and decided to read it again backwards. A few dozen pages later (earlier?) questions started to crop up. I'd been sitting there a while (two hours and eight minutes to be exact) and still there was nothing on the horizon. I don't know if you've ever had occasion to wait in a restaurant while the raving lunatic sitting just at the next table is enthusiastically savoring his *filet aux champignons*. You can't take your eyes away, you watch him eat, you drool, and whenever he chews you follow with the tips of your lips. And if he's ordered something greasy you spend the rest of the evening with heartburn.

"But what's the hurry?" I thought. "My visa's good for four months, I'll probably get served before it expires." As I've said, I am a true devotee of slowness, and believe there is no greater pleasure than taking your time during a meal.

If I were trying to get to the White House, my main goal would be to make life better for my fellow citizens. To do that, it would be enough to convert the country's fast food places into slow food places where people could eat at their leisure. As Groucho Marx used to say: "It may not make their lives last any longer, but it will make them seem longer."

26

OUT TO LUNCH

One thing the scientists at NASA and myself have in common is that we both make mistakes. Of the many I made in New York, one stands out as by far the stupidest. To tell you the truth, I'd prefer not to discuss it but suppose that we must, so here goes. The problem with me is that I can't keep my mouth shut around women. Don't get me wrong. This is not the result of a grotesque overbite. If you must know, my teeth are as perfectly arranged as the keys on a piano, which ought to give you some notion about how my cavities are laid out as well.

That particular day I was browsing around in a department store looking for a pair of jeans my size. The sales clerk was a large dark-eyed blonde, stunningly proportioned. We'd just touched on the topic of my Arab origins when I felt compelled to inform her that save perhaps for an assortment of African ruminants (the impala, springbok, gnu, and of course the gazelle), she had the most beautiful eyes I'd ever seen. The compliment bore fruit. She had a lunch break coming. And if I wanted, we could continue this discussion in the cafeteria on the ground floor.

That half hour break was undoubtedly the longest half hour in modern times. Let me explain. To both her misfortune and my own, Gloria, for that was her name, was about as lively as a snail on thorazine. Don't misunderstand me, I have nothing at all against snails or thorazine. I am merely trying to describe in the fewest possible words the kind of corner I'd painted myself into.

Gloria was evidently a graduate of Higher Nursery School but for want of ideas was obliged to ceaselessly recycle the same sentence.

Her vocabulary was as impoverished as my bank account. The entire range of words she used could have easily been stored in a lexicon of a single page—a page with margins creamy as her complexion, ample as her bosom, and empty as her head. Half Gloria's time was spent batting eyelashes, the other half fiddling with her hair, the other half sniffing perfume samples, and the other half contradicting me (you can easily calculate what an impossibly long half hour it was). Whether I talked about literature, sports scores, world hunger, the stock market, or the recipe for seven-vegetable couscous, her response was always the same: "Hold It Right There Buddy!" She was not writing me out a ticket—merely sharing the depth of her thought, which I'm afraid was much worse than any fine.

I got a two-minute respite when Gloria went off to touch up her face. No other man, however stoical, could have resisted the temptation to slip away. Yet there I waited, a slave to my preposterous notions of courtesy, until her return. In spite of a pot of herb tea and a slug of thorazine my sleep that night was unsettled. Gloria, in the form of a large snail was actively stalking me through a labyrinth of open books, each page as blank as the next.

We all make mistakes at times—it would seem the essential thing is to learn from them. There are several morals to be taken from this story: Some days have it and some days don't; There's no point looking for meat if you're a vegetarian; Even a walking dream can bring on nightmares; And finally, if your need is beautiful eyes, stick with a gazelle!

27

MAIL TO FEMALE

Sunday, 23 August

Dear I.,

Guess what I saw on my walk around Washington Square—a couple kissing on a park bench—nothing unusual about that, but as I drew closer I realized that that short-haired woman was in fact a man. It's the first time I've ever seen a pair of men slow-kissing, the way you and I used to do it. And then, just as I was passing I glanced over once more to find I'd been doubly fooled by the short hair and leather jackets—they weren't two men at all, but two women. New York never ceases to surprise me. Every time I go out for a walk I get the feeling I've had too much to drink.

You wrote about your proposed trip to the South of Morocco. Sounds like an excellent idea! The air will do you good. While you're down there getting your fill of dunes and oases and Kasbahs, don't forget to keep your eyes open wide—you're seeing for both of us.

Affectionately yours,

Tuesday, 29 September

Dear I.,

I got your letter just this morning and am writing back from a stand-ing position. There's a good explanation for that which I'll get to in a minute. Ray invited me to Connecticut for the weekend. It was a lovely place, the countryside there is magnificent. What can I say? The leaves were leafy, the greenery was green, the rivers were wet. Ray and I took some nice walks, we went canoeing, and for the first time in my life I rode a horse! It wasn't a very long ride, but today I'm walking in a trot and if I try to run I merely break into a gallop.

The weekend will stay with me a long time. I'm bearing the scars, in fact. It will soon make a week that I haven't set my rear on a chair, or anywhere else for that matter. Of course, as you're always saying, one should try to look on the bright side. What I've lost in mobility I've gained in etiquette. I give up my seat to the first comer in the subway these days, not just to old people and pregnant women. I guess just rid-ing a horse is enough to make you a knight sometimes.

Painfully yours,

P.S.: I've started to write a book about New York. At the moment it's as incoherent as the city.

Friday, 30 October

Dear I.,

In your letter (13 Oct.) you ask why I'm writing a book. Of course I could say I'm doing it on behalf of the underdog and the dispossessed, to denounce American imperialism, or simply to share my profound reflections on the world we live in.

None of the above. Do you remember that roll of fat around my middle? Well it's been getting bigger ever since I got here. To the point that today the neighbors down the hall were asking why I needed to wear a life buoy just to walk to the grocery store. I've tried everything, believe me—body building, walking, jogging, stretching, even parking (this consists of spending an entire day in a parking garage with nothing around to eat).

And then came the unexpected miracle cure when I got back from Hartford and wrote down my impressions about a boutique for dogs I'd visited. Before finishing the second page I'd lost 300 grams. By the end of the evening I'd lost a whole kilo. Since starting my book I hardly eat at all, and the more bulk it takes on the more I lose. In fact, I've grown so thin I doubt you'd recognize me any more. At present I'm so light that before I sit down to write I have to tie myself off to a twelve-volume encyclopedia, six volumes per side, otherwise I risk flying away (along with my ideas) at the slightest gesture. I estimate I'm losing about 250 grams per page on average. I don't know how many pages the book will end up having, but with any luck it will appear before I disappear.

One last thing—I got the pictures. I don't care for your new haircut. You look far too good in it.

Jealously yours,

Thursday, 26 November

Dear I.,

It's cold. And getting colder. Next door at Olga's place though, Spring seems to have come early. Olga spends her nights serenading, let's say, and each time she sings not only her bed but every piece of furniture in the vicinity beats time.

Make Love, Not War? Whoever the bonehead was that came up with that one, I can assure you he didn't have Olga for a neighbor. Wars end however long or destructive they happen to be. But Olga will never surrender, and I fear I'm going to snap (unless her bed does it first). For close to a week now I've hardly slept a wink. I'm exhausted. If the bags under my eyes could talk, they'd tell you how hard it is to share a floor or perhaps they'd simply express their views on Weltanschauung (I'm too tired to explain, do what I did and look it up).

I miss you. I feel lonely. There's another tremor reaching a crescendo next door. In here it's just lonely. Anyway, greetings.

Agitatedly yours,

P.S.: Here's what I read in my horoscope after I'd written the above. "Nothing too exciting about the vibrations affecting you this week. It's a question of being subjected to persons or situations. Above all, don't count on anyone to act in your place. Trust your instincts. The tiller is in your hands."

Saturday, 5 December

Dear I.,

Just a quick word or two. I can't go on. Olga will not stop challenging men to her duels. Another night, and I haven't slept. I am absolutely drained. I want to die, and if my letters keep coming, it's only because I haven't been able to decide how. I hesitate between throwing myself off the Empire State Building, drowning myself in the Hudson, or eating in the cafeteria down the street. I am confident the food there is revolting enough to do the trick.

As I wait to be served, I send you my love and all the kisses you care to accept.

Desperately yours,

28

COLUMBUS' SHIELD

In the year 8016 A.D. an important discovery was to enable the human race to better understand the bellicose behavior of its ancestors. On October 10th at precisely 1:30 p.m., while exploring a harbor site at the mouth of a river, an eminent archaeologist by the name of Columbus excavated a trove of ancient artifacts testifying to a fallen civilization. The till then buried treasures included: fragments of a crown and torch that may have been part of an immense statue, a magnificently preserved piece of cloth with the word "NIKE" appearing above a symbol shaped something like a crescent, a piece of rusted metal bearing the inscription "YELLOW CAB," and a red sign stamped with a yellow "M," evidently dating back to the McDonald's Dynasty.

But the greatest find of all, dubbed the discovery of the century by the archaeologists themselves, was a small cardboard box on which someone had written in a long-dead tongue known as Arabic the words: "My little shield against Death." The shields in question, three rings of inflatable latex carefully housed within the box, would eventually enable Columbus to put forth this hypothesis: Approximately 6,000 years in the past, the human race was waging bloody war against a microscopic enemy.

29

DESPERATELY SEEKING ELEPHANT

In a text I read some years ago, Kostztolanyi evokes the overwhelming desire he had as a child. His fantasy was to someday pull the alarm lever on a speeding train—not to call attention to any threat or danger, but solely for his personal pleasure. "Simply to watch," he explains, "the locomotive and the iron serpent sliding along at full tilt behind pull up in the middle of nowhere in obedience to the will of the brat that I was. Simply to watch the pale passengers scrambling to the windows, and see the railway men running from car to car frantic to find out what had happened, only to discover that the despotic whim of a small boy was the source of all their apprehension."

The other day on the train back to New York I found myself seated opposite one such adorable little wretch. I was entering a few ideas in my green notebook—impressions that might later be of service for the book I was planning about New York. My neighbor meanwhile, aged four or five, was doggedly straining to reach the alarm. His mother, a false blonde of Hispanic origins was just as doggedly trying to dissuade him. It would not be a good idea, it was against the law, he would have to pay the Man With the Moustache a mountain of coins, a hundred times more than were in his piggy bank, and he'd have to face the ogre (she pointed to me) who dragged naughty children out of their beds and swallowed them whole. I felt obliged to look severe and bare my fangs. But the child was impervious to threat. He was climbing the armrest now to get at the alarm, determined to defy authority at any price.

At that point the boy's mother had the happy inspiration of telling him the following story. One fine summer morning the six blind men of a particular village decided to go for a walk together. Just a few minutes up the road they encountered an elephant. The blind man who touched the beast's legs decided the group had run up against a tree. Another felt the tail. "No," he said. "It's not a tree. It's a rope." The third ran his hand along the elephant's flank and declared it a wall. The fourth felt the ear and supposed it to be a fan. "I disagree. It's more like a club," said the fifth, feeling one of the tusks. The last man grazed the elephant's trunk and spoke fearfully of a large serpent.

As his interest in the story grew, the boy forgot his obsession and was soon asleep in his mother's arms. The story may have succeeded in calming the child, but for me it tripped an alarm. To this day, it has served to remind me that while I may have grasped the parts, I have missed the whole. I may humor myself that I know this town and have penetrated its secrets, but New York will forever slip through my fingers.

SEA DRINKERS

Youssouf Amine Elalamy

Translated from the French by John Liechty

"When you got back to dry land you couldn't even piss straight. The toilet wasn't moving, but you, you went right on swaying. You can always get off a boat: but off the Ocean, that's something else again."

—Alessandro Barrico

". . . Where the fierce old mother endlessly cries for her castaways. . . ."

—Walt Whitman

1

Once there was a little girl whose eyes I can't begin to put in words and whose smile, well, I suppose I could try. But how to begin? Let's just say that when she smiled you didn't sit there acting like it was just a child smiling, no, when you saw her smile you couldn't help thinking that on that particular day it wasn't her it was your whole life smiling at you through those lips and teeth. I can't put it in words, some other time maybe. Which is just to say she was beautiful.

She liked to talk to trees, which didn't talk back of course, but she went ahead and talked to them anyway because you had to talk to someone and say all those things in your head, still a little head but already full, talking to grown-ups, imagine that, a child her age, not even a boy, I guess talking to trees or walls it comes to the same thing. A child?! She's already 15 years old! her mother yelled; it'll soon be too late to marry her off, put in her father. The little girl went on playing but she was afraid of the dark, especially the dark-skinned man they wanted her to marry; he could have been her father if not for all that money God knows where he got it from said her mother, what's it to you? yelled her father, I'll die first the little girl said before fleeing deep into the trees.

Some bent over as she passed, some held out their branches to show her the way to the city. This way, a voice somewhere finally said. You look lost, come, sit down, no here, close to me, my voice is smoked out, get closer so I can talk to you, what'd you say your name was? Come again? A little louder, nobody here but us two, OK Zaynab? And why not Fatim Zahra while you're at it? OK, OK, forget that one. Even Zeyn would go good on you, or why not Zouzou? Now there's a name for you, Zouzou, a nice name and it suits you too, you'd be the first in the house to try it out, but why that face? I'm telling you it fits, slick as a new pair of panties girl! Zouzou it is then, unless you prefer Fifi, no, doesn't grab you? Zouzou either? Well take it from me, Zaynab won't cut it for this kind of work, hell it's just a name, why you want to drag it along behind you? I'll bet you've never driven anywhere before, never even had it out of the showroom, and does it ever show, brand-spanking new! Now, now, don't mind what I say, give us a little smile, let's see what you look like when you're happy; there you go! You look wonderful that way! I know a few people who are going to blow their wads come payday and curse the women they married, god what lips, so beautiful! I'll show you how to put lipstick on without smearing – watch, you run a finger between your lips and pull it straight out, straight out, otherwise you smear all over. Here, put on these heels; don't worry, you'll get the hang of it, hell, you'll be dancing before long, wait and see; you should have seen me the first time! It still makes me dizzy just thinking about it; nothing left to eat back home; with the sky like it was you'd have thought it might have got a little wet, started raining I mean, and we didn't get a drop of water that whole year. All those days and weeks and months waiting for the sky to piss down on us so there'd be enough for everybody to eat and drink all the time, but finally you just say piss on the sky, if there's nothing here might as well go someplace else. Same for you? I know, take your mind off it, hey, if you could see how good you look in those shoes; and wait till you try this, don't wear it too far up otherwise they won't see a thing, shame to hide all that, still nice, still firm, that's called a low-cut by the way; no you won't get cold, hot maybe, cold no, to sell the goods you got to put them on display; but why these tears? Come here, lean on me, put your hand here, down a little, that's better, no one's trying to buy you, only to rent you for a while, take it from me, it's not the same thing; some of them are really nice, you'll see, sometimes it's just a matter of having a drink with them; whatever you do don't say no, do like me the first time, look at the foam and tell yourself it's tea, a little on the cold side maybe and for sure a little on the strong side but just at first, not for long, let them get close to you, think about something else and you won't even see them; something that really gives you pleasure, what's that you say? You want to think about trees? Well that's a new one. Whatever pulls your cord, but the main thing is to let them talk, let them say the words they don't dare say to their wives; you won't understand anything anyway, uh-huh, Spanish, I know you don't, you think they're telling you they love you, that your eyes are even more beautiful than the eyes of their first love, but you'll wise up soon enough to what they're taking you for with those words you don't understand; me, from the moment they pay they can piss on me and make me swallow it for all I care, you'll see, money has a flavor too the strongest there is. Come child, sit down, give me your hand, it's cold, mine too, lay your head here against me, that's right, forget the others, and now, now close your eyes.

While her eyes were closed, little Zaynab saw lots of men come and go, Spaniards mostly, one of them, a photographer named Alvaro had eyes as blue as the sky. They didn't get married, they didn't live happily ever after, they didn't have lots of children. Just one.

2

"It was as if," said Ayoub, lowering his head, "as if life was too small for her, a bad fit."

That morning she'd turned her back on the city and headed for the village, belly cupped in her hands. She walked slowly, softly, as if she feared she might break something or wake someone.

First one step,
                    then another,
                                        then another still,
slowly, softly, to the end and beyond. One should imagine her walking slowly, as if measuring with her steps the distance separating her from her grave.

She stopped to urinate on occasion, to feed the birds or talk to trees. And she stopped on occasion to watch the clouds go by. Sometimes she opened her arms and let herself be pushed along by the wind. She was frail as a stem. Pale as milk. Strange. Like the moon.

The way back. She realized nothing would be as it had been before. That day, just before dawn, she'd made up her mind to go back to die among her own, back home, among the memories and colors of her childhood. Back there, no roads, no cars, no electricity. Just a few houses, some animals, a mosque, and the big square with the tree in the middle that blossomed purple every spring. Back there, only a few steps from the sea, a small village: Bnidar.

On her arrival they undressed her and when she was completely naked in the midday sun, they covered her with a piece of white linen.

The women of Bnidar collected her clothes piece by piece, not to be burned or thrown to the dogs, but to be given to their men who in turn hung them from the top of a mast.

The following Friday just before prayers she delivered in the midst of a perfect hush: the child she'd given birth to gave her death in exchange. Zaynab had scarcely turned sixteen.

All season long Zaynab's clothes floated over the village, higher than the tree in the square, higher than the stork nests, higher than the mud minaret. They floated high in the sky, next-door to heaven.

"So that," said Ayoub raising his head, "so that the shame she bore might scatter in the wind."

The child was called Omar.

3

Omar had very white skin and very blue eyes. He was, said the people of Bnidar, pale as milk, strange as the moon, with "eyes cut from the blue of the sky." The eyes of a Spaniard some said. The eyes of a Christian said others. "*Kif-kif*," said Ayoub. "What's the difference?"

Bright and early every morning Omar left the village, skirted the sandbanks, crossed the fields of cannabis, stopped for a tea, eyed the customs officers, bribed some, steered clear of others, then slipped into the little Spanish enclave. There he haggled, negotiated, bought contraband goods, and heading back the same morning, eyed the customs officers, steered clear of some, bribed others, stopped for a pee, crossed the fields of cannabis, skirted the sand banks, and got back to the village by midafternoon. He walked slowly, softly, as if he feared he might break something or wake someone.

Twice a week he went to the village market to sell his goods.

The rest of the time he walked along the beach following footprints in the sand. Sometimes he stopped, dropping to the shore like a wounded animal. He might stay there for hours, eyes full of tears, watching the waves die.

"He's strange," people said.

"People are strange," said Omar.

4

Ordinarily, Omar liked to surprise the fish flying over the waves, to see the shells rolling in the foam, the seaweed stirring at the surface of the water. He liked to walk along the beach following footprints in the sand. He felt like he was reading, imprinted before his eyes, the fragile and precise itinerary that is life. Stretched out on the sand, he stared into waves spattered with golden lights, until the moment he felt his eyelids droop, then close. That blessed moment when the eye, freed from sight, hears.

The sound of the waves.

Nothing else.

Omar liked all of this. Ordinarily.

5

The blue skies of dark days was hanging up above, and there below, scattered about the sand, a strange kettle of fish. Fish so big they might have been human, God forbid, they look human, dear God, like people, they *are* people! And oh my God, they're our people!

Bodies all over the place, run up on the beach. Black ones, white ones. The sea had not discriminated. They all had their eyes eaten out.

"And so," thought Omar, "dying is not seeing the world anymore."

For a long time he examined those wounded bodies, mutilated limbs, corroded faces, flayed hands, broken lips, and he said to himself that these people would not see the sun rise on Bnidar again, not see the fish flying over the waves, not see shells rolling in the foam, nor seaweed stirring at the surface of the water. They will no longer hear the sound of waves. Never again.

That was the day Omar understood that dying is losing your life.

6

One of the characteristics of human beings is to forget that they are mortal. One of the characteristics of death is to remind them.

Sunday, April 22, just after dark, twelve men and a woman join two smugglers waiting for them on shore. Together they launch a small wooden boat and embark into the night. All eyes are set on Europe only twenty-some kilometers away, there, beyond the fog, wet eyes filled with images of a land where you still find work, where the streets are paved with gold, where the tree of liberty bears fruit.

The wind picks up abruptly. The sea gets rough. A monumental wave rises up. Powerless, the little boat turns on its passengers. Save for the two smugglers, all will be found three days later on the beach at Bnidar.

To get on the boat they paid the dealer from Tangier more than 20,000 dirhams each. Twenty one thousand five hundred to be exact. As if they'd worked all their lives to buy their deaths. And considering how young these people were. So young.

They hadn't even had the right to half a life.

7

I've seen them come and go like this since I started. Men, women, children even. They all look the same in the dark. You can't just take them out in broad daylight so the sun can point them out to whoever. They were all in a hurry to get there without knowing where *there* was. They told themselves the sea isn't all that big, that that's just an idea; others have done it before us; with a little luck and not too much wind and if it's blowing at our backs, maybe they could do it too, it wasn't will they were lacking, that's for sure, and anyway what would they stay here for, what would they find to do here all those hours, all those days, all those months, and all those years after that watching the sea and the sea not all that big after all. And I have to blame myself and tell myself, "It's because of you they set out at night, because of you they won't see another day." But if they get their kicks gambling with death what was I supposed to do about it? What's it to me? I do my job like everybody else. If somebody'd taught me to work the land, if it ever felt like raining on us, who knows, maybe I wouldn't have been out there crossing in the dark. And then again, maybe it's nobody's fault really, just that there lives ran out of life, and don't kid yourself, you can't change anything. Your heart gives out, your body's all broken down, and nobody can fix it anymore: the bullshit your father dumped on you and his father on him, and his father before him; the sea burning out your lungs; die a little more or a little less, you're dying all the same. Don't tell me I could have done something about what happened. It was written out for those people right from the start, that urge to go, to leave everything behind, my boat and not somebody else's, and the sea that night waiting to carry them off. It was all written out; just they didn't know how to read it. And I'm to blame for that? All those heads, those arms, legs, tears, looks, dreams, prayers, all those lives dumped in the water. I didn't force anybody to go. I just do my job. I make the crossing, that's all. It's not hard. Risky, but not hard.

Before this I was into fishing. You feed them a little and they end up feeding you. That's how you get them hooked. But it seems they figured it out somehow: risky but not that hard. They weren't biting any more and you either, not a bite to eat for you either. With those factory boats there wasn't anything left for us, God knows what they told the fish to chase them off like that. Fish don't feed a man anymore, let alone his wife and kids.

Brtal's the one who came looking for me. I was just drawing the boat up and not one bloody fish in its belly. He helped me turn it around on the sand and said, "I've got some fish for you, big like this." He spread his arms wide in case I hadn't heard or was somewhere else. He said, "They come from all over, here, the South, even blacks sometimes, you don't need to look for them, no sir, it's them come looking for you. Good thing you got a boat, it's little, all the same it's a boat, and don't worry, they're all too happy to pack themselves in like sardines, and anyway you've got to do something with this boat; you can't just let it chew the sand like this."

Since then I've been making the crossing. Men, women, children. They all look the same in the dark. I'd have some stories to tell, what with all those eyes glued to my boat. The thing is, I don't get paid to tell stories, just to make the crossing. And am I supposed to blame myself for that?

8

Omar liked to follow footprints in the sand. He felt like he was reading, imprinted before his eyes, the fragile and precise itinerary that is life. That day, he was unconsciously following the trail used by a Spanish photographer and his horse. The man's name—Alvaro. The name of the horse, unknown.

Alvaro was the first to discover the bodies on the shore. First one, then another, yet another, feet snagged in seaweed, and a little further on, just in front of him, a head of long black hair coated in sand: "What a bloody waste!" There, folded in on itself, was the body of a strangely beautiful woman, her right arm buried in the sand like a shattered wing.

9

WATER n. (OE woeter) **1.** Colorless, transparent, odorless liquid. **2.** Heavy, muddy, stagnant, clear, fresh; water for prayers, holy Zamzam water, iridescent in the light, sweet as saliva, salt as tears. **3.** Soaks the land, cuts channels, tumbles over falls, gushes from springs, quenches the cattle's thirst, flows at the foot of trees, makes the fruit grow, dilutes sugar, sleeps at the bottom of wells, fills little girls' buckets, purifies the pilgrim, sprinkles the tombs of the ancestors, caresses the fresh bosom of the bride, welcomes the new-born. **4.** Falls suddenly on those bloated bodies and on his head, Omar's, a million droplets of water when least expected, when he lifts his head and the entire sky is painted blue and there's not a single cloud, not the least shred of cloud in the sky, not *one* of those white heads of hair that dress the sky, and all of them are painted blue, and all their locks are painted blue, and every single hair of every lock is painted blue and it continues to rain up and down the beach, on the fish inside, on the shells underneath, on the seaweed up top, on those bloated bodies, those mutilated limbs, corroded faces, flayed hands, broken lips, and it continues to rain on his head and eyelashes so drenched with rain and tears that he's forced to close them if only for a second, only a moment. That cursed moment when the eye, deprived of sight, hears

> the
> rain
> fall.

Nothing
else.

"When the sky is entirely blue, when it's the color of your eyes and it starts to rain anyway, out of the blue, without warning, it is not *raining* so much as *crying*."

To hold yourself perfectly erect never flinching while all the water in the world is falling on you like that all at once, not bowing your back, not bending your knees, to stand perfectly erect in order not to be engulfed. A million droplets shattering on your head, a million deaf little groans in your wide-open ears.

Omar stayed like that under the rain for twelve full minutes. The 13th minute, when the sky had cried itself out, he started to run towards the village with the image of those water-bloated bodies in his wet eyes, all those children of God who will not see the sun rise over Bnidar again, or anything else for that matter. He started running and shouting—with something like glass in his voice, several pieces of glass, shattered forever, irreparable—running and shouting—the way he was shouting it sounded like he had two or three voices—shouting at the top of his lungs: "They drowned!" and all the echoes in the world repeated after him, "drowned!" and all the voices of all the echoes in the world repeated after them, "drowned!" He started running and shouting the news there in front of himself, shouting and catching up to it, shouting and catching up till it reverberated in Salem's ear—something like a regret, or a rending sound perhaps, and definitely like breaking glass—while he was fishing like he always did at that time of day, perched on the big rock dominating the sea. And Salem repeated after him, "They drowned!" softly, in a whisper, as if to himself. "So as not to scare off the fish," some will say; "Because you know that sort of thing isn't easy to say," will say Salem. And passing in back of him at that exact moment could be seen a private vehicle borne on two wheels of equal diameter of which the rear wheel was driven by a chain that transferred the force exerted by Moh's legs upon two interdependent pedals in opposition. Interdependent like the drowned people on the beach, in opposition like the young and old of the village. And Moh, who was moving through life butt-on-a-bicycle, carried the news along, *like breaking glass.* He started pedaling and saying, "They–drowned– they–drowned!" faster and faster, "They–drowned–they–drowned!" not that it was an emergency or that he was afraid he'd forget, but because pedalling that way, faster and faster, his own heart, Moh's, Moh, Hammadi and Mennana's son and owner of the only bike in a 10 kilometer radius, began to beat, not, to be sure, that it hadn't been doing that before, to be sure, but that it beat harder and harder, as if to remind him that *he* was still alive. And Saadia, who was making pancakes heard him call, "They drowned, they drowned!" Quick, some oil. These better not stick, and considering the kind of shape he must be in about now, if there's anything left to save, it's the pancakes, and she'd told him not to go and inevitably he hadn't even heard her, what with all those waves in his head, it made too many voices at the same time, and if running out on her here like that isn't a shame whether for money or some Christian slut, go figure. And when she was all finished, she'd go have a word next door, once she'd smothered the fire with a fistful of sand, she tells Mina, after rubbing her hands together a few times, she tells her, but not before tidying up a bit, not before that, she tells her: sit down Mina, sit down, not there, here, that's better, you'll be more comfortable here, take this, here, you don't want one? They're made with honey, not sugar, taste one, they're very good, and still hot, go on try one, too hot for you? I guess you're right, we'll wait a bit, not too long though, they're no good cold, no good at all, I forgot to tell you, how's that? Not that, no, I know what she said, I stopped listening to her a long time ago, yes I know all that, I'm telling you, we can discuss it later if you like, here, try one, but now it's cold, what did I tell you? And by the way, they drowned. She says it to her just like that. Like you'd say: "The pancakes burned." And Mina, who was licking her fingers ran for the big square undoing her red scarf, she let down her hair, she started turning in circles. It looked like she was dancing or maybe not. Her hands formed a megaphone that hid her face. It was something to see those two hands rolled up like a shell, and drowning inside way at the bottom a voice that said, "They drowned!" And before long all the people in Bnidar had gathered round her.

And Lfatmi said: "They drowned, the jerks."

And Talal said: "They drowned, the jerks."

And Zakaria said: "They drowned, the jerks."

Not once, but twice, Saadane circled the big tree, the one that blossomed purple every spring.

And Saadane said: "The jerks, they drowned."

"They drowned!" said the men. "They're dead!" said the women. "*Kif-kif*," said Ayoub. "What's the difference?" Even so, though Omar. Even so.

And before long the entire village was on the beach to see the bodies up close, see them with their own eyes, touch them with their own hands, slowly, stirring the seaweed, gently, to avoid getting pinched by the crabs, and then saying, and together saying, and all together saying: "THEY DROWNED!" And this time the cry went up so loud and high that in less than an hour the wind carried the news all the way to the capital, and before day's end, it had been all over the country.

The entire country, within which the northern provinces, within which the village of Bnidar, within which Hammadi's house, within which Hammadi's room, within which Hammadi's radio, within which a man's voice saying: "Two careless swimmers were drowned near the little town of Bnidar."

That's all.

"Two careless swimmers."

Voilà.

11

Talal's oldest, he was the one who came looking for me. He just stood there not saying anything with all those words on his face and trembling hands. I poured him a glass of tea and saw the glass tremble in his fingers. He pretended to drink but he didn't, just touched the rim of the glass to his mouth like someone who didn't like tea but didn't dare turn it down. I kept an eye on him, how he wasn't drinking, and now I understand that with all those words in his mouth, all that sorrow on his tongue, all that grief on his lips, it wouldn't go down. His eyes were fixed on the glass, they were fixed on the glass as if he'd have to swallow the words in there first before spitting them out to me. I heard him say, "They drowned!" and me, "What are you talking about?" "They drowned and Louafi too," and me, "My God, do you know what you're saying?" "They drowned and your son with them," he said.

Talal's oldest, he was the one who came to tell me. Then he emptied his glass and ran off leaving behind those heavy awkward words, with me crushed underneath—too hot because they were too cold, and so sharp most of all. He said they drowned and your son with them. I called out after him, he was already running, the others maybe but not Louafi, the others probably, what sorrow for all those mothers wounded forever, sliced to bits by those cutting words, the others maybe, but not him I'm telling you, see for yourself, he's still sleeping, what's your hurry? Don't rush off, I'll make some more tea if you want, this pot's cold already, see for yourself how my child's still sleeping, lay a hand on his forehead, see how hot he is, put your head there, that's

right, that's it, see how he breathes? Look how he sleeps, head under
the pillow the way he does, sound asleep under the sheet, not seaweed,
not that, the sheet I'm telling you, seaweed for the others. All those
others down there on the sand, what you were saying.

My eyes watched him running in the distance and I heard my mouth
say, "They drowned and Louafi too, they drowned and my son with
them!" I saw my hand close the door after me, and my legs carrying
my body. I saw my feet go forward slowly, very slowly, with tiny steps,
following the sandy path that leads to the beach.

My feet were not running, far from it, might as well die right away,
they merely went forward

with

tiny

steps

like

this

to make the moment back up, and to live a little longer, only a little,
just a little, nothing much but better than nothing. I saw the sand carrying my feet, my feet carrying my knees, my knees carrying my legs,
my legs carrying the rest and my head full of that fire, those words
burning everywhere, "They drowned and Louafi too, they drowned
and your son with them!" I saw my feet moving forward slowly with
tiny steps to make the path even longer, the beach even further, as if
you still needed to walk, pant, breathe, a while before dying for good,
before seeing those eyes that will see no more. I don't remember their
color anymore, my child's eyes, brown or black, I don't know any more,
for now let's say black, it's simpler that way. Later I can check if they're
still there. I know the fish like that part. I keep walking slowly, softly,
to live a little longer yet before finding the others there, and looking at
all that, Louafi's body without Louafi, hand limp against the sand, his
snuffed-out gaze behind the seaweed. To put my eyes inside there and
die with it, and all the days ahead pretending to breathe, to live, eyes
open, pretending to sustain a body that is and is no more, to answer
when someone speaks to me, even to speak myself at times, and find
the right words, avoid the ones that aren't said, all those nights to sleep
through, because it's dark and that's what the dark is made for. All my
life to pretend to wait on a death that's inside me.

The other day he talked and I said nothing. I didn't know what to say to him when he talked about leaving, to find himself over there, on the other side, beyond the boats, nothing but blue skies. His head in his hands, such a big dream for such a small head. And so heavy to hold. His eyes were already away when he talked, his voice too, "You only get to live once, isn't that right mama? You ought to know better than most what it's like to miss the boat. That's right, leave instead of just sitting around here pounding dirt down a rat hole like my father and his father and his father before him, following the course they've laid out for me, only to end up totally lost most likely. Tell me why the land of my birth has to be where I die someday, why the world has to end right there where the waves lay the sea down on the sand? No mama, I won't be some beast of burden with its eyes bound to the land that has stopped feeding it. Yes, leave, just leave, and stop waiting for a rain that doesn't come, a sky that doesn't answer, a life that doesn't grow, and that weed everywhere, don't worry mama, I'll never touch the stuff, I guess I can still live without dealing death, live without turning my back on life, even if at times, you know, you must know, how can I put this, ok, I burn myself to see if I'm alive, I set my hand on fire to prove I'm still alive, and the thing is mama, I'm still alive enough to leave."

Maybe that's what my child died from, drowned in the fire he had burning inside him. No, I didn't know what to say to him when he talked about leaving, I didn't know how to tell Louafi that without him I'd be left here to die for the rest of my life.

12

"They drowned! They drowned!" and all of us we ran up the beach to see with our own eyes because words aren't enough to show things as they are, to hide them sometimes, but not to show them. We ran beneath a sun that had already drunk up all the rain in a matter of seconds. All that water turned to wet sand then dry sand then hot sand then burning sand and us all hopping over it to see with our own eyes and read what the words were crying out, gripped by the fear of seeing what no wind known could scatter, no wave could wash away, no slumber could make you forget, written forever in the indelible ink of destiny. Running.

R   u   n   n   i   n   g.   .   .   .

Running to leave all those words behind, for the words to stop being words at last and become quite simply, a son, a daughter, husbands, lovers, friends, men come from somewhere else to die here. Consoling ourselves by telling ourselves they arrived after all, just not on the right side of the sea or the right side of life. And then all those eyes looking right, left, ahead, behind, then right, then left, desperately seeking among the multitude of signs a detail, something, anything, tooth, moustache, ring, mole, clothing, hair, scar, vein, nose, eyebrow, in short, something to settle on in order to say next, "They drowned! They drowned and my son with them." But perhaps they won't find anywhere to settle. Even after sifting through those little nothings that mean a great deal, and who knows? With a little luck, and no bad luck whatsoever, and all those prayers on the way, and if the doors of Heaven were open that day? Well, not all the way shut, let's say, open enough to receive every word on the lips of this barefoot man, his My God My God My God My God, louder with each step across the sand growing hotter and hotter, no, not his son, still so young, the others maybe, they were asking for it, all they had to do was sit tight and be sensible, you don't mess with something bigger than you, the sea, that's all! Might as well take on the sky! The others maybe but not his son, not this time, not yet at any rate, My God My God My God My God. . . .

But maybe it's nobody's fault but the people's who end up there on the sand, or lost on the ocean floor, drowned in whatever dream happens to be haunting them, wrists slashed, at the end of a rope, a bullet in the brain, all the young people who do that, leave for over there, and stay for good, never again to eat or drink or draw breath here, temporarily overcoming their boredom and satisfying their desire, but those things are there all the time, to the point of obsession, not only when you're suffocating inside them. Maybe those people. Maybe their dreams are a little too big for their britches and their lives a little too small, too tight to wear. All those days and all those nights. All those years of constriction, tearing at your skin, forcing an opening so you can get out, finding yourself over there. To leave, only to leave.

The cry went up "They drowned! They drowned!" and we all ran over the sand to see the words with our own eyes. All except Louafi's mother. She was moving slowly, taking tiny steps, like this, to make the path longer and the beach ever further, so as not to get it over with right away, let him live a little longer, only a little, not a matter of years, but better than nothing. She slackened her pace till it became very tiny, barely visible to the others. Steps so tiny you could measure them between thumb and index finger. Steps like someone saying "no bigger than this," with the "this" being the space between the two fingers, *You're in a book, not in life and not in the cinema; I therefore request that you please be content with words*, and "tiny," that's the only word available, and it's still too large to describe her steps. She stopped now and then to massage her aching knee, that pain that grips her whenever, and last night still, massaging her knee with her fingers to stir up a little life, assuring herself thus that if her knee is, she still is, and all this life like a dress before death strips it away. She prolonged the route that led to the beach taking tiny steps, telling herself the others

maybe but not him, her own son, no, he was ok, just drunk a little salt
water for a change, just tasted the sea to find out what it's like, probably tired from having struggled with the sea, his head against the sand,
to get his strength back. No, he'll be ok, nothing to worry about at all,
not like the others down there, all those bodies covered in seaweed, so
blue, and stripped of life. What sorrow for those mothers wounded by
the sharp, cutting words! All those words that don't pretend, that aren't
just there to hide the truth behind, words that say what's coming next,
words that leave a stain and never go away, words that stick—no point
in scrubbing like that, no water can wash them away, no fear can drive
them off. She walked like this, slowly, softly, unable to remember their
color. The color of her son's eyes. Her baby became a child, then a man,
then meat on the sand. Her baby grown tall, who will grow no more.
Her son. Her life. Lifeless. Her son nevertheless. The body of Louafi
without Louafi. His long hair, his particular smile, his broken tooth one
holiday, a scar no bigger than this in the palm of his hand. Like a new
lifeline. Rather short, this one. She remembered everything but the
color, and if someone had asked her then and there, "What color are
they?" to spring a trap on her, "Your son's eyes, what color are they?"
she couldn't have answered, she merely would have kept walking
slowly, with smaller and smaller steps, so as not to get too far ahead, so
as to make the moment when nothing will ever be like before back up.
And all the days ahead full of pretending to eat and drink, spitting out
water because it's too hot, because it tastes funny lately, and especially
to chew your food well to aid digestion and not end up saying, "That
didn't go down so well." All those hours pretending to breathe to make
believe nothing's changed, that she's still living her life, as the saying
goes, that life goes on, toward death of course, but anyway, as if it was
still possible to live at present, to go on seeing without him, to wonder
at things she saw for the first time. Still possible to open her eyes in the
morning, to say, "What a beautiful day! And not a cloud in the sky, not
a breath of wind!" To close them again at night, since that's what the
dark is made for, and it's essential to sleep well to wake the nightmares
sleeping in her, sleep to wake up the next day and say to yourself, "I
had a bad night, bad dreams; slept bad, oh yes." You should have seen
the unbearable slowness with which she walked. One tiny step in front
of another in front of another, each one as tiny as the next, down that
invisible line leading to her son, laid out for her from the beginning of
time. Counting the steps, one, two, three, four, five, again from the top,

one, two, three, four, five, again from the top, skip the numbers and stick to words, words not totally open, not totally closed either. "They drowned! They drowned and your son with them!" a little like a door ajar with all those words peeping their heads out, but their heads only, foretelling, letting one catch a glimpse of the end of what has been, the beginning of what will be, words that name but do not yet exist because merely audible, not visible yet from this distance, already in your ears but not yet in your eyes. Making one's way there from the other end of the beach, past Chafia's tomb, the trees, the rocks, the hot sand, if hot is the right word for that scorched skin and if scorched is the right word for those feet hopping along on tiptoe, never flat, so as not to get burned. Walking slowly on tiptoe, pushing back the invisible, impossibly fragile thread between speech and sight, Louafi's body without Louafi, limp hand on the sand, snuffed-out eyes behind the seaweed. If only he could see her from where he is, trembling in skin burnt from working under the sun, now that there are just a few steps left before her eyes inevitably light on those words changing along the way from rumor to murmur to echo, to silhouette, to a son drowned in the dream that was burning inside him, draped in seaweed, flung back by the sea. There is nothing so lovely as a mother's eyes resting on her son, her head against his, and not a sound, not so much as a breath to break up the silent show. Even if. There. In earshot. The sea. She's still there. The sea with her music that won't stop playing. But who truly hears it? The sea, fierce old mother of men, recedes.

The mother moves in. Till she covers her son. She bends down with the grace of a dead leaf at the mercy of space.

Like this. It looks like she's praying, and maybe she is, sun on her back and the sea just there, her eyes in his eyes, and in his ears a little, and a lot in her son's voice, still switched on, something still there crackling inside that mouth still full of words that burn, "At times, you know, you must know, how can I say this, ok, I burn myself to see if I'm alive, I set my hand on fire to prove I'm still alive, and the thing is mama, I'm still alive enough to leave." The sea in her son's eyes, and in his stomach. Fierce old mother that took her son from her, that turned his head, drank him down in a gulp, spit him back on the sand. Who dared fight against her? What good to strike at the water? What good to spit at that immense pool of spit? And there. There. All of a sudden. Out of the blue. There. When you least expected it. There. Where you could not have envisioned such a thing (not that you'd never heard of anything like it before), just that, in the midst of all the weeping, the cries, the tears, the pain, who could have imagined this? There, in the midst of everything, a laugh, yes, unmistakably a laugh, not mocking or ironic, not malicious even, just a laugh bursting out like many laughs at once, like a storm on their heads, all that laughter showering down on them, amusing no one, irritated as they are by this woman "who takes it like this," because it's your right to laugh sometimes, of course it is, and it's appropriate when life's not up to its old tricks, not bugging us too much, when it's a matter of something amusing, but laughing—there—that's something else altogether. What about the pain? What happened to the tears? And this mother laughing even louder than the weeping, who says it's only with tears that we weep? Laughing in the midst of all that? Just another way to cry? No less beautiful, no less true, more painful probably, with that biting feeling tickling at your insides. As if she could really laugh at her son's death, open her mouth and let fly, bursts of sharp laughter to cut the silence and the weeping and crying of the others, really sinking her teeth into it, her tongue bitten and bloody. Who could do such a thing? And who could tell us how long this laughter is going to last? Will someone be able to stop it one day? If only she could pull herself together now, if only she could stop laughing and act as if nothing had happened, perhaps then someone could ask her, yes, one might well ask her why she's like this, one might well ask what's making her laugh like this.

13

Who's there? Is that you mother? No, I don't see you. How can I, seeing how dark it is out here. Switch on the sky, why don't you, so a person can see something. What? No, I don't think I've got the strength to wait for dawn, I'm in and out as it is, not far to go mother, not far to go, believe me, it won't be long now. No, I couldn't stay there pretending, I didn't see how the lights were ever going to go on in my life, how any color could ever dress up my days or stars my nights. You know I don't like to play games, mother, you know very well, don't you, how I can't play at being happy, no matter how I tried to hold myself back and lie sometimes, I just couldn't stomach life, nothing to do about it, believe me, I tried everything, all those years pretending to be someone else, someone happy just to be alive, happy to put that face on forever, that body three sizes too big, and too heavy most of all with those kids talking all the time behind my back, "There's Momo there's Fatso there's Momo there's Fatso," those voices chasing me to the water's edge, their laughter on the wet sand and further still sometimes, I had only the sea to turn to mother, she's the one who welcomed me in her arms, who called back at them till their voices were drowned out. I've never felt lighter than in her arms, less heavy even than a leaf, and there's one more thing, no I never told it to you, mother, it's a couple of years ago already, like some aching shame holding you tight, never letting you go. You want to know what it is? No mother, you don't know but I'm going to tell you about it so you do know even if there are some things that shouldn't be said. It was hot that day, the village, you know, was out praying for it to rain, so there'd be enough for everybody to eat. Six months without a drop of rain. Not one. The whole village out on the big square, children in front, barefoot, hands clasped tight, eyes on the blue up above. You had to see those children, had to hear them asking the sky for forgiveness, and me Fatso, watching them from the window, not joining in, no way, I watched them in the plenty of my body, in the insolence of my flesh, and in shame first and foremost, in a body indifferent to want, to need, to hunger, to the distress of others. I didn't see the faces of the men further off, but I haven't stopped seeing them since in my sleep. All those men behind my eyelids, every night, going down the little sandy path that leads to the cemetery. If I could have fed them that day from my flesh, mother, I would have done it, yes I would, from my own flesh. I'd have got lighter at each mouthful, and been losing my embarrassment and shame at the same time. Only with those looks in their eyes, those voices at the water's edge, that laughter on the wet sand forever in my ears—I had to leave. Tell me—who better than the sea to take me in her arms and hold me weightless over the waves? Last night I got on the boat with the others. I didn't know I'd be going so far. I didn't know I'd be crossing my whole life in just one night, mother.

14

There above were the blue skies of dark days, and there below, scattered about the sand, a strange kettle of fish. Bodies all over the place, run up on the beach. There was Momo, known as "Fatso," who that bloody wave caught off guard and who would probably have been eating something at the time, anything, just a little something, and Louafi, known as "Pretty-Boy" due to his long hair, bloody Louafi, always quick to say: "C'mere and I'll show you who's the girl," and Jaafar, known as "Houlioud," the one who couldn't stay another second behind that wall, and Abdou, known as "Midnight," which makes sense considering his skin-color, and Moulay Abslam, known as "Tale-Spin," due to all the beautiful stories he told at night (the one about the man who started writing books because he didn't have any money to buy them with, the one about the kid who refused to grow up because, he said, "You can catch your death of death that way," the one about the woman who read her husband's dreams, she read his dreams all right, she read his dreams till the day someone found out the poor guy talked in his sleep! And the one about the sailor who never got seasick save the nights he set sail on his wife) and Anouar, known as "The Waiter," who died thinking about Ilhame or Ihsane, he didn't know which anymore, lungs filled with water, pecker erect, this big too, what a waste! And Slimane, called "Slim," known as "Bad Luck," an unlucky stab and that woman clutching her cheeks screaming "you're crazy, crazy, crazy, crazy, you're crazy," and Charaf, known as "Stargazer," to go stargazing with him you didn't need to go anywhere, you smoked one and the stars came to you, and Salah, known as "Sbania," the one who wanted to drink up the sea, (that's all!) And Abid, known as "Speedy," who found himself running in the sea with death breathing down his neck, and Ridouane, known as "Assbackwards," that should teach him to let his beard grow when there's not so much as *one* hair on top of his head, and Zouheir, known as "The Mute," because he'd spent his whole life holding his tongue, and,

> a little further on,
> there was,
> folded in on itself,
> the body of a strangely beautiful woman,
> her right arm buried in the sand
> like
> a shattered wing.

15

Chama was. . . .

When you wanted to talk about this woman you'd start by saying "she is . . ." and that's all the further you'd get. You'd say, "she is . . ." and get quiet. It's crazy, you'd rifle your whole head, go through your entire wardrobe of words, they were either too big or too small for her, never her size, there weren't any words for her. Sometimes you'd sit there the whole night looking. You'd spend hours in the dark stringing words together, one by one, like little pearls, and the next day, you'd start off saying "she is . . ." and just when you were going to get her to wear them, the words slipped off, slid to the floor—slipped through your fingers. It didn't make any sense. Not one single word would stay in your mind and you'd be stuck there spinning your wheels, could spend the whole bloody rest of your life there for all anybody cared—nothing. You would not find that word.

Good Lord but this woman was beautiful, and no word, no scent, no color, no music even can ever render that infinite beauty. When she started to sing it was silk. It was pure silk. And when she stopped it was as if all the birds in the world had stopped singing. Nevertheless, if you wanted to talk about her you had to come up with something. So you'd start laughing to cover the silence, or laughing the best you could. God Almighty, it's not possible, there has to be a word, just one, one syllable, only one, one letter long perhaps, who knows, a word, a simple little word to *say* this woman, but it was futile to look, you weren't going to find it, not that word.

You'd see her go along a wall in broad daylight, and on the wall, no shadow. Not so much as the shadow of a shadow. You didn't believe your eyes. Another time you watched her walking, straight ahead, never dropping her eyes. You followed her over the beach and over the sand, behind her, not a trace. It doesn't make sense, I know. Don't try. Behind her, not the least trace of a footprint in the sand. Not one. Incredible. This woman walked without leaving footprints. In which case, you inevitably tell yourself that the word you're after doesn't exist. Inevitably. For if it did exist, it would be so delicate and light, so light and sweet, *so sweet* it would melt in your mouth before you'd have time to pronounce it.

16

Omar, my darling, my prince, my beloved. I tell these words to the sea, I sing to her through the night, I whisper into her ears, so she can report back to you some day. All you'll have to do then is keep an ear out, you'll see, and you will hear me and understand and you will forgive me. I couldn't stay in the village. My father says you're strange, that you're not like us, that you'll never be one of us. And he says it's enough just to see your eyes, so deep and so blue, to measure the gulf between us.

Omar, my beloved, I don't know what time it is, or how much time has slipped by since our departure. Even the boat didn't want to get wet, imagine. You should have seen it clinging to the sand with all its might, balking like an ox being led to the butcher's. That was a sign my companions couldn't read, me either, blinded as we were with the urgency of leaving. But that's no longer important; just now I've got all eternity before me. Eternity minus a day if I can hold on to this board a few more hours, and beat back the cold biting my legs, the hunger burning my insides, the froth stinging my lips. But nevertheless, I sing and sing sing, never stopping, I sing to the child you planted in me and that death's come looking for. I've given him a name, Gabriel. The name of an angel so far as I know. I know he hears my voice, louder even than the song of the sea, the despair of men, the fury of fate, I sing to him, sing, sing, sing, because to die in music, I believe, is to live a little more, and because to die in music, I believe, is to die a little less, I sing in memory of my companions lost in the belly of the sea, in memory of those she's about to feed on, in memory of myself as well, for you must know, my darling, my prince, my beloved, I'm worn-out, cried-out, just a wisp of voice left to sing with. And she's there looking me straight in the eye. Everywhere. In this board I cling tight to, in the breeze whipping my face, in the sky up above with its silver eye, and the cold and the thirst and the night and the sea, of course, the sea who's not quite done rocking me, to help put me to sleep no doubt. She'll get the better of me in the end now that I'm in her arms, I know that. Then I think again of you and feel like I'm drowning in the blue of your eyes, letting myself be carried away by the flood of your tears. Know that nothing will ever again be able to take me away from your gaze, not even the darkness when night falls. I'm yours forever, with you, in you, part of the air you breathe, in the sand under your feet, in your wildest dreams, in the heat of your desire.

My Omar, who loves to watch the dying waves, you'll be walking along the shore and see me spring beneath the foam. With each wave I will become a dove, will unfold my white wings, will bow as you pass by, will glide up to lick your feet with my perfumed feathers.

Omar, I long to find you again. Bird, fish, foam, shell, seaweed, who cares, I'll be there, I will wait for you.

And so in closing I look forward to hearing from you again, but I'm dead tired, I've got to turn in.

17

Sunday, April 22, off Bnidar. No more than a few minutes. Ten at most. On the horizon, a sun wet to the shoulders. The sea sizzles slowly. Up above, the sky takes its leave in a red gown. Only a moment. Darkness reaches the beach. Taking tiny steps. Night holds its breath. And here's the moon, round and full, climbing the dark, slowly. Softly. She observes them with her blind eye, shadows fleeing in the shadow of night, towards that boat balking with all its might, they're tugging it furiously over the sand, like some beast that fears water, clings to the earth with what strength its got left, obstinate, stubborn, strange steed that gives in at last, overcome by immense fatigue. It feels them climb on its back, glides over a wave, and in water to its waist, slips to the open sea.

Midnight ride on the sea's back, nothing more by this time than a vast desert of black sands, save to Abdou, known as "Midnight," (which makes sense considering his skin-color) the only one who knows how to write; for him, the sea, this immense expanse of ink enough to fill entire books, mountains of books piled one on top of the other, kilometer on kilometer of ink thread to say the world and love and joy and fear and trees and flowers and little birds, and the big ones too and fish and life and hope and dream and day and night and the sea, of course, the sea not quite done rocking them in her arms, to help put them to sleep. Once and for all. Beneath her foam coverlet. She dances in the dark, fidgets, gets impatient, loses her calm. Then all at once breaking loose on those children and on that beast, strange steed lurching one way then the other, drunk with pain, worn down, no choice but to drink the sea, all those waves attacking in the night, closing in from all sides, relentless, tearing its flesh to bits—pitiless, insatiable—till cracking the beast's bones, drained at last.

A monumental wave rises up. Powerless, the little boat turns on its passengers.

All those bodies crushed under the weight of a wave and emerging, one by one from the belly of the sea, water to the neck, and more to come, eyes on the stars, fear in the stomach. These boards on the water, a miracle, a blessing. Everyone clings to life, to those pieces of wood. Keep on floating, that's the stuff, never stop floating, don't give up whatever you do, breathe in, that's good, keep breathing, moving, ignoring the cold that bites your feet, then your legs, then your stomach, then your chest, don't let it climb too high and get you, hold your head up, that's the way, good job, keep your eyes on the stars, whatever happens, don't fall asleep, think out loud, remember, image of a woman from someplace else, that first meeting on the beach, the white linen cloth she was wearing that night, and it was like embracing the moon, heart dancing, butterfly drunk with light, rendezvous with love, in the shade of an almond tree in bloom, this skin like silk, never having touched any in his life, silk that is, those kisses under the rain, her eyes in his eyes, "My love, my love, forever forever . . ." the wedding went on three days, what an adventure! Birth of the baby, a feast day . . . and the cold goes on biting your feet, then your legs, then your stomach, then your chest, don't let it climb too high, don't fall asleep, remember or better yet tell stories, that's the thing, tell Moulay Abslam's stories to the night, the one about the man who started writing books, the one about the kid who refused to grow up, the one about the woman who read her husband's dreams, the one about the sailor who never got seasick . . . no, not that one please, forget the sea, stop thinking about it, "My love my love, forever forever, my darling my darling, forever forever, my darling, my darling, forever, forever. . . ."

A woman turned shadow in the liquid night, she who'd never cast a shadow. Not one. She continues to look straight ahead with nothing there to see. Simply trying to believe. She clings to her piece of wood with the little life she has remaining, and a mother's love, still stronger than the waves and the cold and the pain and the night. If only he hadn't been there. If only. She would have raised her hands to the sky and let herself be swallowed up. No regrets. Her eyes on the stars, like a last prayer, she would have given herself up to the sea. She holds on furiously, if fury is the right word, not for herself but for him, the little angel sleeping in her, unconcerned, if he knew, her child, her little one, but he does not see the night all around and will doubtlessly never see the light of day. The child's death came looking for him in his mother's womb.

The roar of waves and a voice singing in the dark. God of sky and earth and sea, this woman is singing. Incredible. Beyond all comprehension. She's not screaming, she's not yelling, she's not even crying. She's singing. That's all! Singing when death is looking you straight in the eye. It takes a mother to do that. You can't imagine the sort of thing they're capable of at times. She sings, never stopping, never even letting up. With the strength of a hunted animal. She sings to drown out the noise of the waves, and that of the wind, and that of the man crying "mama, mama, mama, mama, mama, mama," (someone wants to call his mother, let her come, she can't be too far off now), and another lifting his voice to God above, mainly so as not to be misunderstood, he has never stopped praying, never missed a Friday prayer, not even when the desire for his wife was stirring his belly, he who, true enough, did not always share all he had, but frankly, what did he have to share? he who abstained from eating before sundown during Ramadan when the others (a curse on the others) hid behind the wall to eat fruit, fruit that wasn't all that fresh maybe, but fruit all the same, he who took off just like that without saying good-bye wanting to see his kids one last time still, them holding a hunk of bread with that look children have when they're eating, he who gets impatient and protests and makes express demands on Him, although He's in an ideal position up there on high to see how cold he is, how afraid he is, how hungry he is, how he is in pain.

A man clinging to a board. Water to his neck. He holds the board between his hands. He snuggles close to it. He runs his fingers again and again along this piece of wood that speaks to him through the night, a woman's voice, his wife's—a beautiful wife, yes, very—*Come, put your hand here . . . , Look what I have for you . . . , Just a quick feel . . . , Look Ridouane, round and full the way you like them . . . , Do you want me to say those words that are not to be said?*

The sea is out of breath. Recovers her calm. And this woman still singing. Beyond all comprehension. Never letting up. To the point of becoming unbearable. A torture for the others, gripping pain, never letting go. If only you could let the board go and block your ears. But might just as well let go of life. She sings, sings, sings and doesn't let up singing. Unbearable.

"Shut her up somebody, before I strangle her!"

"What with, pray tell?"

"You saw her hair didn't you, how long it was, that long hair of hers?"

"You talking to me?"

"No, the girl."

"C'mere and I'll show you who's the girl."

"Easy, Louafi, easy."

"Abdou's right. Shut up and pray."

"Yeah, like the sea's just the spot for doing your prayers."

"My uncle says that in Casablanca they built this mosque out over the sea especially for that."

"Sounds like your uncle's doing a little too much dope, don't you think?"

"Jaafar's right, it's like you're so far out over the water you could pray and catch fish at the same time."

"What the fuck would you know about it? The only thing you ever caught is a an old shoe. And no laces either. Get real!"

"Since when's it my fault people throw their shit in the sea?"

"That stuff about the mosque is for real. They say that to get it built, everybody helped out, everybody dug as deep as they could."

"More like somebody dug it out for them as fast as they could."

"They say that just by giving a dirham you buy yourself a place in Paradise."

"Yeah right, you couldn't even get one in Hell for that."

"My uncle says the minaret's so high you can touch the sky from up there."

"You're uncle's really full of it, isn't he? Sounds like he's got his head in the clouds."

"Why am I even telling you this? You can't even ride your bloody mule."

"Well for one thing, I don't have a bloody mule."

"How about the one you ride on every night?"

"Easy, Louafi, easy."

"Mama, mama, mama, mama, mama, mama."

"What's he bawling about?"

"Anyone care to call his mama?"

"I'd say if she's dead, she mustn't be too far away at this point."

"Mama, mama, mama, mama, mama, mama."

"Shut him up somebody, before I strangle him!"

Clinging to the same board, men talking. All but Zouheir. Zouheir, he doesn't talk; he keeps quiet. Quiet for the sake of being quiet. What's the use talking? What's the use? You can spend your time talking, saying any word you like, you can line them up just so, one after the other, for hours on end, you can talk just as much as you want, silence is always going to get the last word. So what's the use?

A wave rises out of nowhere, taller even than a tree. Men swept away in the current. Cries, weeping, arms, legs, a chest skewered on a piece of wood, wounded bodies, mutilated, torn, and this man lifting his hands to the sky as he slips into the sea's belly. Noiselessly. *This guy tells such great stories! Tell a story Moulay Abslam, tell a story,* he'd have a heap of stories to tell now, *One more Moulay Abslam, just one* God knows the stories he'd be able to tell, *One last one Moulay Abslam, just one last one for heaven's sake*, and this one might even be the loveliest ever. But what's the use of starting a story if you can't finish it? At that, he slips into the water, and his stories along with him. All those stories, all those words drowned on the ocean floor, piles of words, thousands of words, words of every imaginable color like little fish in the water.

Somewhere in the world, their faces burned by sun and sea, sailors will draw their nets in full of these strange fish. They'll tell the full story of that journey, without ever having made it themselves. Does it matter? Their eyes on the sea then on the sky they will speak of these men without even having met them. In order not to forget. They'll spin a tale with tears in its voice from the words they'll have caught.

The story of these men and this woman who found death where they were looking for life.

18

There were times the moon would be coming through the window, and I'd close it to keep the light off me. Not that I don't like the moon, but it's better without it. And that way, even with nothing on, the dark is there dressing me, my head, my feet, and not only. . . . Otherwise I couldn't look at him, you know, or look at myself afterwards either. How's that? No, no, no, Moulay Abslam, not my husband, that loser didn't last long, he couldn't even make babies, but as for the rest, well, you know, I'd rather not . . . Moulay Abslam? No, I didn't marry him, come off it, he could have been my son, it's true, I'm not kidding, count them up and figure it out for yourself. Yes, him too. Me, loose? No, not really that, just that sometimes I feel a little funny, I don't know, kind of emptied out inside, and there's nothing like a man to fill the gap. Only once or twice since. I mean since the other one left. A couple of men, that's all. Well come to think of it, maybe three, I'm not that sure any more, probably because it was dark. I'd shut the window and wait for him. I'd leave the door open. Often, I wouldn't even hear him come in. Through the door I mean. I don't know whether I should really be talking about all this. Maybe a little later. Here in all this light the words don't want to come. Let's just say he did certain things to me and afterwards I'd shut my eyes and sleep. Not like those nights I'd spend tossing in bed chasing off the words in my ears and the pictures in my eyes, smacking the pillow, not that it had done anything to me, just that something had to take the blame. Afterwards, when I was sleeping, my dreams made me do things I never dared do. Not me.

Not to him anyhow. No, not even in the dark. I'd shut the window to keep out the noise and most of all to keep in the silence. Just his body against mine, his breath on my skin, and nothing else, not even words. It was like that each time, never any different. You could ask him yourself if he was still here. He kept perfectly still and I kept perfectly still and the world too behind the closed window, not a word in the midst of it all, not a single word would come to say the things we were doing. We just did them. With our arms, our legs, and all the rest. And that's when I understood. How can I explain it? But I'm not sure I should be saying it in the first place. It took me a while to understand it myself. I guess I can say it to you. I'm not so sure you'll understand, but I'm telling you all the same. Well, never mind. Here goes. I understood, I understood that happiness, I understood that happiness, that that's where it lies. In silence, not in the words that drive it away often as not. Now I know that sometimes, no, many times, maybe even always, we speak in order not to say things. All these words in your mouth and then in your ears, like a veil or a wall or merely a burst of laughter to hide certain things behind and say the ones that aren't. It for sure wasn't words Moulay Abslam needed, what with all those stories he used to tell. Often even. He wasn't at a loss for words, not him. Every color imaginable. Blue ones to cry with, soundless white ones, pitch black ones, and even red ones full of hate and blood, and sometimes love. And all those words that used to follow you everywhere, the ones that went on speaking to you behind your eyes, in your sleep I mean. Speaking to you all night, and even later, in life. This is how Moulay Abslam used to go about it. He'd ask you to pick a word, it didn't matter which, just take the one on the tip of your tongue, and he'd turn it into a story, a whole story, fabulous and beautiful, very beautiful, strange even, painful sometimes. Just one word, one only, that he'd uncoil and then use to spin a tale and you could rest assured it would be one you never heard before, and you'd start believing what he was saying, you really would, you yourself would have believed it. Zohi believed it anyway; he let himself get taken in like a rat in a word trap, even though he knew better than to fall for that story about the virgin widow, you know the one I'm talking about, you don't? Well then you're the only one who doesn't. Zahi fell for the virgin widow, that's exactly what he did. It's true you'd have to be a little . . . you're right there, but these things happen. The fact is, they happened to him. Trapped, like a rat. He started loving the widow in the story, and even afterwards, in life, and every evening that Moulay Abslam brought her to life for him. He lost his appetite and his eyes, his eyes you know, they stayed lit up. Even at night. With the fire burning inside him. Until one day Zahi told him, he was obviously at the end of his rope, "Make her die, Moulay Abslam, make her die so I can sleep!" That day he chose the word "end" and asked him to unwind it. To the bitter end. To the rest, he told stories. To me, he did things. Not nasty things, mind you, but I'd rather not discuss it just now. You'd need the words to do it in the first place. He's the one who had them, not me. And when the rest were saying, "He tells some really fine stories, that guy, some really fine stories, that Moulay Abslam," me, I was thinking "he does some really fine things." And I knew what I was thinking about too. Every night a new cruise, and me getting on board the bed with him, a little like putting out to sea. Not that I've ever been on a boat in my life. On a bed yes but a boat no. I've only been told. I've been told that from up there you can see the world waltzing away and the village with it. You're right to think I never went on one myself. Except maybe when he was doing things to me. All those nights rowing together on that rocking bed, and me caught in the middle of the waves. And all that wind taking me away from the world, bringing me closer to that shore where I went to die a little each night. And then one day he left and never came back. You don't come back from the kind of death he got into. He used to say that his stories, all of them, it was the world telling them to him, and he, all he did was listen. I know it sounds strange. I'm not sure I really understood even though he explained it to me. You, you look at a tree and you see a tree, trunk, branches, leaves, a tree. Him, he looks at it and hears a story. Strange and beautiful. Who knows how he did it? Lately he'd been saying how he had to go and leave the country, that the world here wasn't talking to him anymore. He was listening but he couldn't hear it. He said that he couldn't breathe anymore without the stories. Couldn't face himself anymore. Couldn't even do those things to me in the dark. Would you believe, it was like he was doing those things with words. Awful! All those words in me, all those stories between my legs. I don't know what it means. Like I said, I didn't really understand. I only know they found him on the sand. That's right, with the others. A curious tale. Strange but not beautiful. Not beautiful at all. You should have seen what they looked like when they found them. Now I know that even without him I'll go on breathing, eating, drinking, even sleeping. But never living. Because, you see, since he's dead—I know I can tell you these things same as to myself—and so, you see, listen closely here, since he's dead, me, at night, in my bed, I'm not dying anymore.

19

A room at the top with a view of the sky. April night, past eleven. One of the town's smaller hotels. Red rug on white tile floor. On the rug, an open book, two bare feet, a black spectacle case, a pair of glasses, various photos, and on the photos, the eyes of a photographer.

1. Sea bird in foreground. At rear, folded in on itself, a woman's body. The bird stares into the lens. Like it's posing.
2. At bottom left you can make out a head of long black hair coated with sand. It makes you think of a desert plant from this angle, or a piece of burnt toast. Unusual picture. Not much else.
3. High angle shot over a woman's body, her legs "dressed" with shellfish. Small blobs of sunlight emphasizing structure of legs. Low light, much more so than usual, intensifying the purple coloration on the face, lending life to the subject, so to speak.
4. Another angle: portrait of a sea monster, half woman half plant. Very low sun furnishing the necessary relief. Contrast in textures comes out particularly well. Really fine.
5. In foreground: undulating sand, contour of an abdomen, rounded shoulder, slope of a breast with nipple on top taut as the bud of some flower.
6. Long hair. Again black. A man's this time. Shadow on the lower part of face gives the impression subject's wearing a mask of light.

7. Variant showing man's body laid out in opposite direction. Light on lower part of face gives the impression subject's wearing a mask of shadow. Photographing a dead person presents at least one advantage, as you're dealing with an inactive subject who's obliged to stay in the field of view. The inconvenient thing, of course, is that the dead don't pose.

8. An enormous blue blob in background. The sea in this one's nothing more than a chromatic presence, a backdrop of color, no more, no less. A wide aperture normally blurs the background, but also permits sharper focus on the eyes. Providing of course that the subject still *has* eyes.

9. Close-up of a man's hand, a silver ring around finger and the pincers of a crab around the ring. Looks like they're trying to take it off. Or not. Oblique light back of the creature rendering the most minute details visible to the eye.

10. A part of the shoreline draped in seaweed, blue as far as the eye can see in background. Diffuse light softens the color of the drowned man. A Senegalese or Malian. Or just some black perhaps. To photograph a drowned person of color, it sometimes helps to adjust your exposure a stop and a half. Using a light meter you'll get more control over how much light you want on the dark skin and avoid overexposing the background.

11. The sea blends into the sky on this one. Blue completely fills the picture. "Saturates" it, as we say. One gets the impression that the birds are flying in the sea, the fish swimming in the sky. It's very beautiful. Very. Documentary interest: none whatsoever.

12. In the distance, two small red stains on the sand, like two drops of blood. You can't really make out two bodies from here. On the other hand, the sea comes out so cleanly it's practically detached from the sky.

13. Variant using a 30 Red CC filter. This time, it's like someone's diluted the two drops of blood in the sea.

14. Used a 24mm wide angle. Selected aperture gives an adequate depth of field and allows one to separate the bodies from the sea in background. Positioning the camera *at ground level* gives the impression the bodies are floating on the sea. The ideal surroundings, naturally, in which to photograph drowned people. The sea, moreover, makes an exceptional backdrop with its palette of blues and greens.

15. Completely blurred. Something wrong with focus or overexposed. Or both at once.
16. High angle close-up of a man's face partially covered in seaweed. Mouth Seaweed-free, strange expression there. Like he's trying to say something.
17. Extreme close-up of mouth. Lens focused practically on top of it. Making face fill the entire frame.
18. Variation with tiny shellfish just emerging from mouth. Another split second I'd have missed it. Pure luck.
19. Here the horizon cuts picture into two perfectly equal halves. Undulating sand and foam from the waves illuminated by lateral light on lower half, and on upper a morning sky rendered a deep blue thanks to polarizing filter. Presence of bodies on shore messes up the unity of the composition. From a *purely esthetic* standpoint: they're in the way.

Various photos on a red rug, perfectly arranged one behind the other as if on an imaginary set of tracks. Like a little stationary train with strange passengers on board. Some cars contain sand, some death. The ones in the middle carry the sea.

The eyes of a photographer. A rug on the tile floor in a room at the top in one of the town's smaller hotels. Past eleven. April night.

The following Wednesday, above one of the 138 negatives taken that day, a French weekly runs the headline:

WHAT A PRETTY LITTLE BEACH!

20

Some pieces of paper for keeping an eye on the world. So as not to let it get away. Some photographs to say things with, to say what was. Giving you something to see and taste, a small bite at a time. Till you feel sick. The broken arms, smashed legs, hollowed-out eyes, bruised faces, cut flesh, burned skin, staved in chests, torn hair, the remains of Momo, Louafi, Jaafar, Abdou, Moulay Abslam, Anouar, Slimane, Charaf, Salah, Abid, Ridouane, Zouheir, Chama. All these bodies picked off the ground, one after the other, first of all leaning over them, next bending your knees, above all getting them centered right. All these bodies turned into pictures, that will never finish dying under our eyes. All these images, so they won't slip away. Never again at any rate. Staying put. Playing dead. Motionless. Forever. Being there when needed. Letting them rest their fingers and eyes on you, because they've got to get their fingers and eyes on something to be able to say afterwards that they've seen and that now, inevitably, they know, they too, even though they may still be ignorant of all the things that will stay smothered behind these images forever, mute because invisible, invisible because unfathomable. If only one could truly capture this man in the blue shirt and blue pants. It's clear enough in the photograph, anyway, that they're blue, though some of the blue's bled away in the wash, nevertheless still blue enough for one to say they're blue, not totally white yet in any event. Something like the sea with all that foam. Yesterday, today, and still tomorrow. If only one could understand this man, hands on his shirt and pants, almost blue, not totally white, just getting his feet wet, carrying the color of the sea so later she can carry him. If only one could hear the voice of this strange and beautiful woman, strangely beautiful, singing words like silk, without ever having touched any in her life, like pure silk: *"My love is pure as water from the spring, may my true love slake his thirst with it."* To start with that and nothing else, a song louder than the others to drown out the noise of the waves, the wind's blast, the cries of the men. If only we could see this man endlessly rubbing his hands together, to get all that blood away from his eyes and those words away from his ears, "you're crazy, crazy, crazy, crazy, you're crazy." If only we could see the boat they're tugging furiously over the sand, balking with all its might, with what strength it's got left. If only we could see those men emerging one by one from the belly of the sea, eyes on the stars, fear in the stomach. If only we could feel the cold biting feet, then legs, then stomach, then chest and climbing too high and getting you in the end. If only we could hear that man shouting in the darkness "mama, mama, mama, mama, mama, mama." If only we could read the words buried in Zouheir's body, swallowed over an entire lifetime, drowned in an eternity of foam. If only we could see the face of this woman leaning over her son still so blue, so stripped of life, her little one grown tall, who will grow no more. If only we could see this mother walking slowly, with tiny steps, in order to live a little longer before seeing everything, the body of her son without her son, limp hand against the sand, his snuffed-out gaze behind the seaweed, and his voice in her ears forever, "You've got to know, mama, I burn myself to see if I'm alive, I set my hand on fire to prove I'm still alive." If only we could hear that.

If only.

If only we could see all that.

Then we might begin to understand how we could have seen the pictures without seeing a thing.

21

I guarantee you it wasn't me who took the pictures. I swear it wasn't me. Jaafar here, the drowned guy. The one chewing sand, with seaweed all over his back. All because of the wall. At least that's how I see it. They called me Houlioud at the factory. Hollywood. That's where I lived. It was this place on the outskirts of the city, full of sheet metal shacks. Not the sort of thing for rich folks, I admit that. And yes, just the sort of thing for poor folks, I admit that too. But that sheet metal was home for all that. Sometimes there'd even be words written on the metal if it wasn't rusted out. Words we didn't know how to read. I put mine up just before the others started doing the same. It was a good three and a half, maybe four meters long, and at night when you were sleeping, you could really stretch your legs. I guess I had big ideas. I kept telling myself that someday I'd find a healthy wife, young and not too beautiful, we'd make some kids, I'd watch them run around awhile, and then I'd get old and I'd shut my eyes.

I put up the first place in Houlioud, just before the others started doing the same. Then came Chiadmi, Amimir, Laarej and all the rest. There wasn't anything left to eat back where they came from. It seemed like somebody'd sent the sun just to drink the water out of the sky. In the end they didn't even have any tears left over to cry for their animals. Whole families come to harvest the misery and sickness and bumper crop of bullshit that grows in this city. Welcome to Houlioud! That's what I'd tell them.

If they were young, their wives could still find work. On the other side of the tracks. They spent their time cleaning the piss off the peckers of kids who could hardly stand up yet, polishing the toilet bowl till it turned white as Monsieur's ass, putting red flowers in place of the yellow ones to make Madame happy, she thought it was prettier that way, up till the day they had to be let go because they took some sugar for their kids, or dared to push away the hand Monsieur was fondling their butts with.

And then one day some men paid us a visit in Houlioud. Driving a blue car. I mean blue like the sky at night. It drove off the blacktop and came up to where we were. With a trail of dust running along behind. Old Aflouh stood up and gave a military salute. But then he'd have saluted a dog the same way. He fought in the war, and I sometimes wonder if he ever came back. At first they came in pairs. To get an idea what we looked like. There was one who kept pulling at his pant leg and another always looking at his watch, checking to see if it was still there. Their skin was whiter than ours without the dirt. They both had black eyes and looks to match. And suits blue as the sky at night. One of these days I'll get me a set of threads like that. I can get suits by the kilo if I want at Uncle Sam Rahmane's. He's called that because he's got used clothes "Made In You Say" as he says. And he says it often enough. Every Sunday it's there on his shirt, the one with the stars shining all over it.

The two blue suits were there to take measurements. They did the whole tour of Houlioud, from the first shack to the last. The next morning workers started building a stone wall. A solid wall, too. Out of solid stone. Najah's son was the first to notice. He was all red from running so fast. We all went out to see with our own eyes. I've got to say it, nobody'd ever built anything for us before. All day long we watched them working, sometimes right up to dark. Like they really wanted to get it over with.

The first time I was with Laarej, Bnini, Hrizi, and the widow Hogga. She'd spent her entire life in a hospital holding a rag. Mopping up somebody else's blood. She looked at the stone and said:

"You know what that is? No, I don't guess you would, look at you sulking there, you spend your time opening and closing your mouths and think you're saying something, but you're not saying anything, not anything worth a crap anyways; I'll tell you myself if I have to, I'll tell you what that is, just keep it to yourselves though; it's a hospital, that's right, you heard me Jaafar, and you Laarej, and you Hrizi and you too Bnini, you can wipe that look off your face, think I don't see you? A hospital I'm telling you, not a cemetery, not that at all. How's that? You're right, it is the same thing, they lay you out on a bed the better to see your life bugger off through the window; I watched that boy die, he wasn't more than ten or eleven, death under his skin and in his eyes, still as wide open as ever; he was watching his life run off on giant steps. I saw him go, not a sound, not even a bandage to dress his wound with, just my eyes to cry for him, my voice the only cure around; I talked to him about the earth, the valley and the mountains and the wind and the rivers too, and I saw him go on over to the other side, a little scrap of life left behind, next to nothing, nothing much anyway; he raised his eyes one last time as if to show the way or I don't know what else and he left and with him all my joy and laughter; I said you can wipe that look off your face Bnini, Hrizi, and you there; no, you don't know, you spend your time talking and you think you know; I'll tell you myself what that stone's all about, I may be only a woman, but I've seen grown men cry, men tall as a tree, as a tree, you hear me, men burned by war, and some it had kept a little souvenir from too, an arm, or their legs, or their faces; I don't think I've closed my eyes since, I really don't think I have, or if I've slept I don't remember anymore, or very little, not enough to fill up my nights at any rate, I'm telling you they were tall as a tree; today I share my bed with their arms and their legs, rinse my mouth with their tears, wash my face with their blood. I wake to their screams. You want the truth? Well, I'm going to give it to you. Sure as there's a God in heaven, boys, that wall's a hospital.

"Me, I say a school. You just have to look at all the kids hanging around her to figure that out."

"Why not a hotel while you're at it."

"No way, it's a mosque, I know it."

Hrizi was very familiar with the city's mosques. He didn't go there merely to please God, rather because there was bread to eat morning, noon, and night. Not always the freshest bread perhaps, but bread all the same.

It took the others a little more than a month to build their wall. At the end, one of the workers said "That's that" and they left. It was about four meters high, the wall was. There weren't any windows and no roof either. Just a white wall going around Houlioud. Because on the other side, you see, there were people in their cars who could see everything. The kids in their dirty clothes, the sheet metal, and whatnot. We weren't ashamed, that metal was our home. But it was different for the others. A wall isn't such a big deal, I guess, but I couldn't go on breathing anymore behind it. That's how it is.

And that's when I decided to leave. Over there. On the other side of the sea. That prick in Tangier took everything I had. To get anymore he'd have had to rip out my teeth and sell them back to me, the little bastard. But I just told myself: it doesn't matter, Jaafar, it doesn't matter. Afterwards, in the water, some guy was calling "mama, mama, mama, mama, mama," as if his mother could hear him, and then this woman singing in the dark! Incredible! She wasn't screaming, she wasn't crying, she was singing. That's all. It was her way of dying. When I saw that wave in front of us, I got one thing straight in a hurry. It's like this, if you're not born on the right side, there'll always be a wall to hold you back. It might not be made of stone, but it will be there all the same. God forgive me, I shouldn't have said that. So let's just put that I didn't say anything.

22

Ridouane's face bathed in moonlight. Night all around. A woman's hand on his beard; on his head, not so much as a hair, and *in* his head the sea. She's there again that evening, clinging to his dreams, unwilling to ever let them go; dancing continuously before his eyes, in her blue-daubed gown, loosening first the foam fringe, then removing it, loosening it once more, again and again, a step forward, a step back, a step forward, a step back, not really retreating, the sea, not really advancing, dancing continuously to the bleached-out music she holds the secret to, the music of silence some say, but making an infernal racket all the same, and he's the only one to hear it just now, like a call flung from beyond the ocean, if only he could ignore it, forget this voice that won't ever let him be, won't ever let him go, always there roaring through the night, a spell, a conspiracy, God knows what all, she will never stop speaking to him in the night, wherever he may go, poor man, whatever he may do she'll never let him be, not for a second, until he goes to join the others on this beach of grays and blacks to get on the sea's back together, insatiable monster, and poor Ridouane, who knows firsthand the kind of racket she makes in his head, impossible to ignore it, useless to block your ears, what's the good of trying, it doesn't work, you don't cheat on the sea, there's no stopping that sound, not worth putting his fingers in his ears, only to wake the sea that has always been sleeping inside him, and this woman beside him, how can he tell this woman, his wife—and a beautiful wife she is—how to explain the sea to her, can she ever understand? *Come, put your hand here. No. Not tonight.*

CHAPTER 22

Look what I have for you. Please, not now. Just a quick feel. No, please no. Look Ridouane, round and full the way you like them. Not tonight. Do you want me to say those words that are not to be said? Some other time. That's what you always say, tell me, how to explain the sea to her? How to tell this woman? His wife—and a pretty wife she is—she who doesn't understand anything anymore, who's had it up to here, and not a single tear on her face, what's the use? But even so she cries at night, her big eyes open, noiselessly, she'd have so many things to tell him, God knows what she'd tell him, a thousand questions jostling in her head but only the one spilling over at present:

"So, what's she like, the slut?

"Blue."

"Her eyes?"

"No, blue. Entirely blue."

23

If there hadn't been all that blue in front of him he'd have done the whole thing on foot. No forests to cross, no mountains to scale, no cliffs. He wouldn't have even had to ask directions. Just walk right on over, straight ahead, the sun on his back, never looking back. There, in the distance, under a gray sky, was Spain—*Sbania!* Every day he saw it scoffing at him behind that immense blue turban, and if it hadn't been for all that water, he'd have gone there on foot.

Face to the wind, eyes riveted on the sea, Salah waited. Alone, feet in the water, he waited. He stayed there motionless, watching the waves run, wear themselves out, and come die at his feet. After hours and hours of waiting, he crouched down, plunged his hands in the water, and drank. He'd dip a little out each time, day after day, however long it took, drop by drop, he'd get to the end, not right away of course, but one of these days, and that would be the day he wouldn't so much as say good-bye. He'd turn his back on the village and go over on foot. How to forget him standing there, how to forget the face of this man who wanted to drink up the sea?

And then one day—one night actually—this voice speaking to him about a small wooden boat, you climb on its back and it on the sea's back.

"Don't worry, Saleh, trust me, there's this boat I know will drink that thing up for you in one gulp. Cross my heart. Just a few hours. The whole sea. Down to the last drop.

Strange sight this woman bent over her son, all blue and stripped of life, but her child nonetheless, big hands and feet, but her little one nonetheless, a week's worth of stubble, her baby nonetheless, that she took in her arms for the first time, just the other day, as if it was yesterday, God how time flies, thirty years this winter, no forgetting that night, the storm, the pain, the rain, the blood, and this child smaller yet than her arm and still all red just out of the womb, and whether to call him Mohammed like everybody else, or Brahim in memory of your father, or Hammad after mine, or Jemaa, since it was on a Friday, or maybe even Abdelkrim in honor of our hero, or why not Salah so that he'll be good and proud like you. Salah, that's the one, yes, her little Salah, Salah her baby, with all those waves coming to lick his feet, that seaweed on his legs on his arms on his neck, his flayed hands, his broken face, his wounded eyes; she runs her fingers again and again through his hair, caresses him with her cheeks—strange sight, this woman bent over her son—she holds him in her arms and hums a little tune in the hollow of his ear, as if he could still hear it, she sings him a lullaby with what's left of her voice, like old times, as if he wasn't already asleep enough as it was:

Poor Salah, poor little thing, you wanted to drink up the sea.
Poor Salah, poor little thing, you wanted to drink up the sea
and the sea ended up drinking you.

24

Here, take this. I didn't count it but you can see there's quite a wad. I'd never had so much money before in my whole life, and if these hands could talk they'd tell you they'd never had so much either. There's nothing but the sea to wash all this blood away from my eyes and sleep. I shouldn't have gone there, but maybe that too was written. Same as with my work and everything else. There's no getting around it—things are different when you're working. You feel like you're somebody then. I'm serious here, not just talking to hear myself talk. I didn't used to walk like this back when I was going to the factory. But there are times life forces you to hang your head. Not that I don't know how to be happy. I can laugh my ass off if I feel like it. It's just that I don't feel like it much. I felt like it a hell of a lot more back when I had a job. No matter what you got hanging between your legs, you're not a man if you're out of work. Jamal says it's like prison, the bars may not be there in front of you but they're inside you all right, and they won't let you breathe. Something happened to him, he couldn't move his arm anymore. One day you can move it, the next you can't. Nothing to do about that. Just one of those things. Like your arm died ahead of time, wouldn't wait around so you could all kick off together. Jamal's boss just told him "What good's an arm if you can't even use it to wipe your ass?" which was another way of saying he'd lost his job. As if losing his arm wasn't enough. I still say if you're out of work you're not a man. That's a natural fact. Even Adam up there in heaven had that figured out. And he wasn't born yesterday. He'd about had it up to here just hanging around in the Good Lord's garden. You can't spend your whole life picking daisies and listening to the birdies sing. So when the little lady handed him that apple he ate it. Of course he did. Just to get some work. I really understand that guy. I mean I really understand him. Me, I'd spend my time eating apples too if it meant getting my job back, but deals like that don't happen but once, and then only when you're not around to take advantage of them.

I should have known better, then again, maybe that was written too. They were all there calling out "Hey Slim, the boss wants to see you Slim, the boss wants to see you!" It took balls to go through that door. As for him, he didn't even look at me, just told me he was thanking me. I wanted to say, "You're welcome Sir, just doing my job," but the other guy grabbed my arm and said, "You don't have a job anymore, are you deaf or what?" Some things I'll never understand. You could give me another lifetime to try, it'd be the same thing. Lbatoul understood right away. That's how women are. You think they're stupid and next thing you know they're explaining things you can't understand yourself.

The first time, I was in a café full of empty tables just waiting for someone to come in and sit at them. Fate is something else, let me tell you. It must have taken her at least twenty years to find that chair, but that's where she parked it, right in front of me. I'm pretty sure that was written too. Of all the cafés in this town, she had to come to that one. With all those bracelets playing their funny music, in case you were thinking about something else, or you hadn't seen them. And it wasn't quiet like before either with that red lipstick screaming on her lips, that dress up to here, those legs hurting you from looking so hard. A dress with big yellow flowers on it. Yellow or red. Orange I guess. Like a flowerbed on her skin and you felt like watering it too.

I shut my eyes. Because her legs were hurting me from looking so hard. A little like somebody tickling you, only with fire. And you're burning all over. So I shut my eyes. To put the damn thing out. Somebody explained it to me once. When I was little and the world was a little too big for me. There was no mistaking it. "When life is hurting you, shut your eyes and put it out." Only once you'd seen those legs they stayed lit and just went on burning you. That's all. I tried looking somewhere else: at the menu up in white chalk, the photo of the team in their green jerseys, the waiter's red shoes, the blue and white checked tablecloth, the two lovebirds in the back, the man's striped shirt, I'd seen him somewhere before, or somebody who looked like him. I tried acting like she hadn't come into that café with that orchestra around her arm and that garden on her skin. Like I wasn't there trying to put out that body burning me all over, like she wasn't sitting in that chair that would still have been empty otherwise, waiting for someone to sit down. A chair with four legs instead of six. I told myself that she'd probably seen a man or two in her time. And I told myself that as sure as there's a God in heaven, legs are made for walking. But if that's all they're for she wouldn't have needed all that, would she? You're the one with the eyes but it's her legs watching you.

I took my coffee and drank it down straight. To the last drop. Like someone who's not used to coffee or who's in a hurry to finish. I looked down into the black of the coffee and drank. To the white of the cup. Just like that. Without stirring. From the bitter black to the sugary white. And I started thinking about the first time I ever ate figs. It was the neighbor's wife who served them to me. I guess she liked me quite a bit or maybe it was me that liked her. I was just a kid really, but already pretty eager to taste some fruit, her fruit I mean. I pulled the black part away with my fingers and licked the red with my tongue. That's how I'd seen somebody do it once. It was like sucking a flower with all that honey burning my lips and again today here in the café. I looked at the flowers on that dress and they weren't flowers anymore, they were figs. Laughing, their mouths open. Their jaws on fire. Yellow and red fire. Orange I guess. I looked at her legs looking at me. I told myself if those legs ever had a notion to take me in their arms I'd surely appreciate the favor, and next thing life would be flowing all over whether fruit was in season or not.

When I think it took her over twenty years to find that chair. It's something else, all right. I made a couple passes through the café, just with my eyes. Then I lowered them and saw red. It was the waiter's shoes, and him in them too. He had his hair combed back and a moustache like the guy on TV. She ordered a tall glass of juice and me another coffee in a little cup. She opened her lips and I saw her teeth. So white you'd have sworn they were new. She wore glasses that were like big eyes for hiding behind or to turn off the sun and I don't know what else. Which is why they're called sunglasses. She looked in her purse and didn't find what she wanted, it was dark in there due to the glasses. She took out a notebook full of names I could have read if it hadn't been shut and if I'd been to school, some pictures of kids or people who had once been, a make-up mirror for when you felt like drawing on your face. All of a sudden I understood what she was look-ing for, even if she, she didn't say anything. Not with words I mean. A little like me who was staying quiet holding back the words that wanted to speak. We stayed quiet for what seemed like a long time, those play-ers in their green jerseys watching us. That calmed us all down quite a bit but not to the point of absolute silence. First you'd have had to get those legs to hush up somehow, and the red lipstick on those lips, and those bracelets making their funny music. And that was before her glass makes up its mind to slip from between her fingers. It probably couldn't take being fingered like that. She, she was all wet, the juice was running between her legs. She leaned over to wipe it up and I saw her fruit. Like the neighbor's only fresher. They weren't figs either, or if they were, I'd never seen any that big before.

I leaned down over her and handed her my paper napkin. I said, "Miss?" she said "Yeah" I said "Can I say something?" she said "What is it?" I said "You're going to be my wife" she said "I'll be your wife if you're man enough." I didn't hesitate a second. I could have, but I didn't hesitate. I turned around and stuck my fist into the first guy who came along. I'll bet the poor guy still doesn't know what hit him. She said, "I hope you've got something as hard as your fist" and we got married. I didn't even have to talk to her the other day. She picked it up right away, about the job and all, just from my eyes. Women are amazing. I hadn't even got around to explaining to her what happened and already she'd found work in a hotel.

Lbatoul wasn't like that before. But after, I'd have to say she changed. She was wearing shorter and shorter dresses and those legs were hurting you more and more from looking at them. I knew of guys at the factory who'd show off their arms to get work, but showing off their legs, never. And always people in the neighborhood going around talking. So you couldn't sleep nights, staying up till dawn because of that. With those bloody figs grinning ear to ear. You know how people are, they're all the same, always looking to stir up trouble.

"Did you know Slim's wife works in a whorehouse?"

"That's not true, it's a hotel."

"Same thing, asshole. Kif-kif."

Those first few days, I was telling myself it doesn't matter Slim, people at those hotels are used to seeing women's legs. That's how it is, you end up telling yourself what you want to hear when you don't have an answer to your problems. So that's what I was telling myself those first few days. Just because she doesn't smell like a sardine and she's got the legs that's no reason to . . . that is, it doesn't make her. . . . I mean that's not enough to make her out a. . . . Not automatically. All the same, I really wanted to know where she was getting all the money. Here's you, a man with arms like tree trunks and you can't even pay for a pack of smokes. And then Lbatoul was smelling awfully good those last few days. And yes, she always came back tired. But did she ever smell good! When you slept beside her it was like lying in a bed of roses. Trouble is she was always tired, work and what not. You could lie there all night long trying, but you weren't going to be picking any daisies, if you see what I mean. The other day I told her, "You tell me, Lbatoul, is it true what people are saying?" and she said "You know how people are, always trying to stir up trouble." Just because you never went to school doesn't mean you can't read, you know. Me, what I was reading in her eyes was all false, even to the point it looked like the stuff people were saying in the neighborhood. You can lie all you want but your eyes will still tell the truth. Seriously, that's the God's truth.

The next day I went to see her at the hotel. I'd never set foot in the place before. What business did I have in a hotel with legs like mine? I could have gone down to Fatman's for coffee, or maybe even stayed in the bed that still smelled like Lbatoul. But I went to the hotel to see her. And see with my own eyes. Because other people's eyes are not enough. Very likely that too was written. My mother always says "What's written is written." My mother can rattle on sometimes, but she got that one right. You can't erase the words the Good Lord's written out for you. They're there and they're waiting for you. And you can't read them. You can study all you like, not just this year and the year after and the year after that, but every lousy year you've got left, and you'll never read the words He has written for you.

I could have gone down to Fatman's, we could have played a couple of hands and he could have accused me of cheating again, or maybe if nobody'd called out, "Hey Slim, the boss wants to see you Slim, the boss wants to see you!" I'd still be at the factory and everything would be like it was before. Lbatoul wouldn't smell so good maybe but she'd belong to me. Nobody but me. And then again I might not have pushed open the door to that room. See, a door's not that big a deal, you tell yourself I'm opening it, I'm not opening it, I'm opening it, I'm not opening it and when you do open it you can't close it anymore. He was on top of her and he was trying to pick some daisies if you get my meaning.

To do that to me. Picking daisies between my wife's legs. Only that. My own wife.

I could have broken his face with my bare hand except it isn't the word "hand" that the Good Lord had written for me but the word "knife." A kitchen knife, you know the type, for peeling things with, not too big, but still enough to open somebody's gut. There was blood everywhere, even in my sleep at night. And Lbatoul clutching her cheeks screaming "You're crazy, crazy, crazy, crazy, crazy." I just looked her in the eye, took the envelope on the table, and got out of town. Here, take this. I didn't count it but you can see there's quite a wad. I even bought some apples for the crossing. You never know.

25

Let's take it again from the top.

This is the story of twelve men and a woman. The woman is pregnant: twelve plus one makes fourteen. Fourteen characters crossing the blue in the black of night. Fifteen, with the little wooden boat. Sixteen, with the moon observing them from her blind eye. Seventeen, with the moody sea. Eighteen, with the fruit basket. Nineteen, even, counting the worm on board an apple.

Let's take it again from the top. This is the story of a worm on board an apple in a fruit basket on a little wooden boat on a choppy sea beneath the blank look of the moon in the company of twelve men and a pregnant woman.

From the top. This is the story of a white parasite on board a red fruit in a yellow basket on a small blue vessel on a black sea beneath a white eye in the company of thirteen gray shadows of which one, it must be remembered, is expecting a child whose color is not yet known.

Evenings when they weren't busy working, the men of Bnidar got together on the big square. There, around a glass of tea, they'd spend their time talking and falling still. All but Zouheir. Zouheir didn't talk at all. Zouheir was quiet. Yes, he was quiet, and how! Try as you might you'd never hear him, even if you stayed there all night long. That's why he was called Zouheir "The Mute." It wasn't that he didn't know how to speak or couldn't—not even that he got tongue-tied. He simply didn't speak. Period. Or to be more precise, he didn't speak anymore. "The fact is, he's got nothing to say," said someone who, while he himself had something to say, didn't know what he was talking about.

As a boy Zouheir had followed his father to this same square and seen him speaking to the village men, gesturing broadly, using the voice that frightened him sometimes. That evening he'd seen his father speak, hold his head, and fall in the middle of the crowd, immobile, struck down by God knows what, a single bolt from the blue, as if he'd got one of his own words down the wrong throat and choked on it. Little Zouheir saw his father speak and die, as if he'd exhausted his words and his life simultaneously, a little like actors who go off once they've said their lines. From then on, Zouheir became Zouheir The Mute, and when the men of Bnidar got together on the big square to talk, he was quiet. Not a single word left his mouth, convinced as he was that one's words and days were numbered, that in saving his words he was saving his life. And yet that day he was asked whether he wanted to go along on the crossing, he said: "Yes." It wasn't anything much, he didn't launch into a string of sentences or anything, he just said "Yes", one word, one only, and doubtlessly one too many. The last he was ever to utter.

Here he is on the sand, quieter than ever, stiff and cold, one body among others, but easy to recognize in his blue pants and faded shirt. My little Zouheir who grew big, but will grow no bigger, seaweed on his body like splashes of garden, and *in* his body, thousands of words drowned in an eternity of foam, kilometer on kilometer of sentences rolled up inside, legible but unread, a giant parchment swallowed up and sealed forever, words swallowed one after the other throughout an entire lifetime, piling up by the hundreds, one on top of the other, all those words he should have shared with the people of the village, and the ones he should have said to his mother, and the ones he hadn't dared say to the woman he loved, words, the words, those words, he repeated over and over each night in the dark and dreamed of breathing in her ear someday, simple words sweet as the dew, like little kisses to place on her brow, but which he will never utter again. Ever.

My little Zouheir on the sand, mouth half open, like he was trying to say something. And still nothing coming out of that mouth unless it would be the tiny shellfish soundlessly emerging, pausing a moment for the camera, disappearing beneath the seaweed, mute.

27

The others call me "Midnight." Because of my color. Or just because it's simpler that way. I don't have a job anymore, or maybe I never had one to begin with. The other day I went to see the sea. To forget everything. And get things off my mind. She was there calling me in her blue dress. I looked at her and said to myself: Good Lord Abdou, why don't you go on over, just to see it, and see what the world's like; it's right there in front of you; just a little water to cross, what's keeping you? There are boats for that, good Lord, you can't spend your life waiting on someone to find you a job.

I remember how all 236 of us, 236 qualified graduates, slept together. Right down town. That's where we decided to stage the sit-in. Right in front of Parliament. "The House of Representatives" as it's called. Which is what we were in a way, we were representatives too. Only we didn't have a house. Not even a roof over our heads. Just sky and stars and a couple of night watchmen to keep us company. Sixty-four days in all, watching the people watching us. Men, women, children, even dogs. Once a little girl handed me a children's book. A story about a tree that can't go on planted where it is. I can really take off with a book, it's like a little window on the world. Or I'd watch this woman. She was my little secret. I didn't know her but still we were together day and night, joined together in the holy bonds of unemployment. I gave her a name: Yasmine. The name of a flower: the jasmine! When she'd go for a walk I'd follow slowly, keeping my feet in the exact places she'd stepped. That was my way of touching her. Of caressing her. I saw her crying sometimes. Noiselessly. I wanted to follow her tears the way you'd follow a river upstream, and get lost in her eyes. Forever.

I watched without saying anything, all the words in my mouth and on my lips refusing to speak. I didn't feel like going into details—the sleep that won't come, burning memories, words that fall flat—nothing to do about it, not worth trying—shame, boredom, and all the rest of it, those images in my head, that face you've got to put on and wear and still recognize in the mirror somehow; God I look like my father, the nose, forehead, his look too; those photos all crying out together that nothing will ever be the same as before; the class picture with me up front wearing my brother's white pullover and my father's look, both still a few sizes too big; the portrait with that speck already in my eye, nothing really, just a black stain in the white of the eye, and that voice repeating: it's a birthmark, a sign from God, a mark of destiny, you'll see, a great man, God's truth, little Abdou, a great man.

Somewhere along the way and still now the image of that woman on a color poster of Spain. Each day her smile behind the glass repeats a little more forcefully that life is good over there, anywhere but here. No, I don't feel like telling this stuff to Yasmine—that I'm sleeping less and less, hardly at all, not enough to greet my dreams even, how one after the other the days are depositing death on my bed, how every day I slip back a step, and while I may have been somebody once, to-day I'm nobody, I don't exist anymore, not much anyway, just enough, unfortunately, to let them go on saying I exist. Black thoughts under white sheets, all those nights in this useless body counting the hours separating me from day. All those days pretending, trying to look like somebody, clean shirt, pressed trousers—not a wrinkle in sight—shoes shined—not a speck of dust on the polished leather—hair neatly combed, a smile now and then.

No, I wasn't going to tell Yasmine how I hit the streets and head for the Ministries, always the same way, walking straight on, following the crowd, even quickening my pace like somebody in a hurry or who's expected somewhere. Somebody at least. Somebody using his shoes to get to work and back. I wasn't going to tell her about this mania of mine for adding blue to the sky, green to the trees, gold to the sun to convince myself everything isn't black, notwithstanding the blank whiteness all around me, newspaper between my hands to hide my face, to avoid the others.

The red polka-dotted cloth drawn over my shoulders, my face in the mirror, the speaker on the radio, his voice on the shelf, his talk I no longer hear, the barber's hands on my hair, his questions at my back, me not responding, like somebody who's busy or who's got better things to do. And all those lines I rehearse in bed, hear myself saying to help me pretend and not to acknowledge all the time on my hands with nothing to do, counting the tiles on the wall, the black spots on my skin, the cars in the street, the pinafored school girls, the blue-uniformed cops, to beat back the boredom perhaps and the shame most certainly as it weighs down harder on my nights and days as well. Shame that is stripping me naked, a little more each day, a lot more sometimes.

No, I didn't feel like telling her this. So I watched her, Yasmine, and said nothing. I watched her, that's all. Sixty-four days watching her cry without being able to follow her tears upstream to get lost in her eyes. Then, to break us up, they promised us a job and I never saw her since. Except at night in my thoughts. In her blue print dress. Blue flowers the color of good-bye. The following month I got an authorization from the Ministry to go teach children. Somewhere down south. The bus ride took all day, and most of the night; the big bridge, the river valley, police checkpoint, the potters, the white houses with their blue shutters, oranges piled at the shoulder, the police, touch of sun on landscape, animals eyeing the grass that wasn't growing anymore, the police, small mud villages, the windshield full of the empty road, the police. . . .

All day, and most of the night. They were all there to watch me get off in my gray trousers and gray pullover. It made them smile when I said I was the new teacher. There were even a few who laughed out loud. Someone pointed out a big stone. Like the base of a statue. "There's your school," he said simply, and this time they all started laughing like mad. I'd seen some schools in my day but never anything like this. An inaugural stone for the groundbreaking ceremony. One day some officials came down to set it in place, taking care to get everything on film so the folks back home could appreciate the Ministry's efforts. Afterwards, they forgot to build the school. I checked my authorization paper. Someone had signed it all right. Someone who'd forgotten they'd forgotten to build the school.

28

I'm cold. My head, my arms, my legs, my feet, all over. Even the sea's cold here, you might say. If only I could run a little to warm up, like I used to. Whenever I ran I'd always come in first. From the time I was little, not just later. Every day would be a day at the races with the Lfatmi boys, Moussa and the others. From the first house to the wet sand to see who'd come in first that day, and every time, there was only one winner and you don't need to waste any time looking for his name either, not worth busting your brains because he was still the one, the one who ran faster than the rest and won every time making you wonder what he had in his feet or head to run like that, no, don't waste your time looking because it was me, and from the time I was little, not just later. I crossed the village, sandals in hand, to the beach and finished the race hopping over the sand so I wouldn't get burned. You didn't need anyone to say who'd won and who'd lost. The sea was the one who decided that. You couldn't cheat on her. She was there and she didn't move. There waiting to declare the winner. When you got to the sea you couldn't go on, you still had the strength to run a little more, but what the sea was telling you then, what she was telling you with her blue words, was that your feet had run out of track, that it was all over, for good this time.

I'd spend hours watching the men pull the boats out and turn them around on the sand. And more hours still observing those wooden beasts come from the depths of the sea, dead tired, exhausted, motionless in their sleep. The next day we'd take off running again, the others behind and me in the lead. Pretending to see who would win.

CHAPTER 28

Over the years I kept running, often alone. I kept telling myself that the faster I ran the better my chances of outrunning myself, that with each stride I was moving away from myself, leaving my self behind. With every step. Carried away by my illusions, that's how I ran, the desire to go far, and further still, the ambition to become somebody. Over there. There where the sea turns back to sand then earth then road. Someone to pay me for running, for coming in before the rest, for never letting anyone pass me, to clap afterwards and hang a gold medal around my neck just for that. I was wearing myself out but never managing to wear out the dream in me, stuck to me, unwilling to let me go. There was just the sea at the other end. The sea saying it was over. That I'd won.

Now I know I always lost, same as the Lfatmi boys, Moussa and the others, I never won, not once, not a single time. I've come to realize that getting to the sea first was my loss, that the closer I got to her the further I got from my dream. I realized she would always be there to keep me from leaving, from going further, that you'd have to go over her first, keep running in the water, long strides, striding along with your arms—feet I can handle, but arms are definitely not my cup of tea—*swimming* it's called, and you'd better be a fish for that, or a boat, or a bottle, or a piece of wood, or maybe just plain nuts, like all of us tonight in this shivering sea.

I really and truly believe that if I still had life some life to run, I'd spend it running, never stopping, never once in my life, I'm not talking about an entire life, here; I've already gone part way, I admit, less than my father and his father and his father before him no doubt, but more than this child in its mother's womb. I have a feeling he's going to miss the gun, but then, the prizes aren't all that great, there's not going to be any winner this time anyway, some other time maybe. I'm tired, worn out. And I'm cold. From my head to my arms to my hands to my legs to my feet, all over. But I cling to this board, I cling to life; I go on running after life, death breathing down my neck. I'm hearing footsteps.

29

Nothing really. Next to nothing. Just a sort of notch above my lip. Everybody says I was born with it, so now I say it myself. A big notch like a hare lip or beak with some strange bird behind it. My father says (he works at the post office—letters, envelopes, that sort of thing), he says the good Lord shipped me out that way so nobody'd get the parcel mixed up. I guess it is like a sort of package with me inside and the women around refusing to unwrap the thing. I don't exactly turn the ladies on, far from it. Otherwise, I would have noticed. From the time I started working in our neighborhood and watching the women watching everybody else.

The other guy at the post office, my dad's friend, he took a look at me and said with that on my mouth I was going to go far, really far. He even said that later on in life I'd be somebody, not run of the mill like all the rest, who didn't enjoy the bonuses I had. Somebody big, really big. He read it on my lips even though I didn't say anything. Nothing you could have heard with your eyes anyhow. He ran his hand along the back of his neck and frowned to say it, in case we weren't taking him seriously. I counted my steps the other day to check it out. I left home and walked straight. I followed my footsteps down to the light, crossed the street, went into the café. Café Salam is where I work during the week and Sunday. Sixty-six steps. I counted. Not one less. Sixty-six with legs like mine. I'd go far was what that guy said, really far.

I do know how to count, and not just on my fingers. Even if I didn't follow much at school. Not that I'm any stupider than the next guy,

I just didn't follow, that's all there was to it. Except when we got this substitute, Miss Ilhame or Ihsane, I don't know which anymore, wearing a different dress each time and always packed tight with her breasts and thighs. I'd never seen tits like that in our neighborhood. A little like Rahal's daughter's, but whiter and not near as much mileage on them. For the first time ever in school, I started following. Oh yes, and did I ever follow! Back and forth across the rostrum and sometimes in her seat. Her legs on that wood and my eyes full of everything, even at night on my pillow. A different color every day, black panties on Thursday, or maybe even nothing, just the darkness between her legs. She left and I gave up on school or maybe it gave up on me, whatever. But I do know how to count, addition, subtraction, and all the rest. Before I didn't but I do now. Since the boss explained it to me. Addition is when a customer gets coffee and a couple of doughnuts and a bowl of soup to finish off. Subtraction's something else, not that hard but hard enough. The boss caught me by the arm and said: it's dead simple, when you break a glass you get subtraction at the end of the month. I caught on right away that me and subtraction weren't going to get along too good. They'll be calling out: Hey you, when's it coming? Is this coffee for today? But me, I go easy, I pay attention to what I'm doing. Otherwise I'll be stuck buying glasses at the end of the month. Broken glasses served up in a mop.

At Café Salam I wait tables and mind what I'm doing, and the rest of the time I scrub. I sweep, I mop, and I scrub. I do it every evening to let off steam. I scrub. Ashes, sugar, coffee rings on the tables, stains on the floor and in my eyes and my nights. I scrub to make it go away, so it can't stay, those kids with their cars and their big mouths, their little girlfriends, boobs up front, hair in back, their eyes behind the windows and us others down on the sidewalk looking at them not looking at us; I scrub and scrub, scrub to make that all go away, and not leave anything, remove it all, the women who don't see me, the children whispering behind my back, my lip in the mirror, still today and forever after, I use a little soap and I scrub, to wash it all out of my eyes, I let my hand slide, caress the tables, walls, floor too, I scrub it and scrub till it turns into that secret flesh, delicious, moist, soft as a breast, white like at school, on the rostrum and especially on the chair, Miss Ilhame or Ihsane, I don't know which anymore, white like inside her thighs with that black stain that won't go away, stubborn, resisting under my hand that scrubs every evening to let off steam.

Every day there was this man at the café behind a pair of glasses. White ones, not the black ones for hiding yourself. They made him look like someone who'd been to school a long time. We get a few of those in here. He was always the first to arrive. I know because he'd come in when the floor was still clean, still not a grain of sugar or a coffee ring on the tables. He'd hold back a second and take a couple of turns around the place, before sitting, book in hand, at the same table as always, under the swinging clock and the king who never stopped watching us. The same book in his hands, the one with the yellow and blue cover, and always on the same page. It's strange, I know. Every day he was there reading the first page in the book, eyes on it like for the first time. His finger on the line, it looked like he was crushing the words, he was pressing down so hard. He lost his son in the war. Only twenty-four and already at ease. He was just starting the book when someone came looking for him with one of those faces that said there was something wrong. Since then he reads the same words on the same page of the same book, beneath the swinging clock and the king who never stops watching us. And then one day, out of the blue, he slid his finger towards the bottom, then to the side, and he turned the page.

I still remember because that's the day the clock stopped. Year after year swinging away, following time's footsteps, to say when it's time to close, pick the kids up at school, have a smoke, call the other guy, buy the paper with the crossword, put a bet on numbers 4 and 9 and 3 . . . and then one day, nothing more. The clock stopped. At four thirteen. Not twelve. Not before, not after. Don't try to figure it out! You'd need to be a clock to understand it, or just a wristwatch maybe, who knows.

I didn't sweep that day. I didn't do the mopping up, didn't clean either to let off the steam. I didn't empty the ashtrays. I didn't wipe off the grains of sugar or coffee rings. I didn't use any soap or scrub the floor. No. I just took off my apron and left. Over there, by the sea. One day a clock chooses to stop, a man decides to turn the page, and me to leave. That's how it is. That's all there is to it.

30

Two or three little clouds and a bird. Way up in the sky. Wings float in blue, then white, then blue. Its flight has the grace of waves and lightness of wind. It writes words with its wings, all on the same page, but we don't know how to read them. Just a bird in the sky and, on the sand, a man who doesn't see it. Omar's eyes are on the sea. Filled with wind, his shirt has the look of a gray sail, almost white in this light. He isn't singing, he isn't resting, he isn't remembering, alone, on the sand. He isn't even dreaming. No, he sees the waves being born then watches them die. From his eyes they swell in the distance, soar skyward, bow, bend down, glide up to lick his feet. Then the waves, all of them, set out again, one after the other. His eyes follow, taking hold, then straight ahead, on to the end of the sea, down that blue highway to the sky.

His eyes in her eyes, Omar watches the sea.

Because the waves are that too, the sea's face leaning towards you. Sometimes Omar closes his eyes and often he opens them, softly though, then closes them again on the sea sometimes, very softly. He opens them and observes the wave unable to run another step, stopping there, out of breath, tired, exhausted, just there at his feet, as if he'd had something to do with it, as if he was able to bring the sea to a stop on the strength of a mere glance. He liked that, Omar did, that precise moment where the sea stops, draws to a standstill, catches its breath, and it's at that very moment he, at that very moment that, it's there that he, that he, he raises that head, his head, his own head to see the sea, see the sea, the sea, at that very instant, see the sea leave, over there,

go away from here and leave, to come back again afterwards, never a
farewell, just a see you later, him knowing she'll come back again, inevitably, not to worry, because it's this too, the sea, this ancestral dance,
always the same, one step back, one step forward, one step back, one
step forward, and all the winds of the world in her sails, that shuddering
body, that wavering destiny, that hesitant voice, I go there, I don't, I go
there, I don't, Omar wants to understand the sea, he wants to listen to
what she has to say and what she says, she who never stops traveling,
back and forth, round trip, here then there, what the sea says, what she
incessantly repeats, is leave and always come back again, retreat but
never run off for good, leave *and* come back, over and over, yes, that's
the sea, the dance, the song, the symphony of perpetual return. And
then let's face it, she can't just stand there, arms crossed, motionless,
can't stand around doing nothing, because she's got to move, got to
struggle to work, the sea, that machine for turning out waves, and why
not go ahead and say it, for turning the heads of men as well.

Omar watches the sea, his gaze bobbing noiselessly like a small vessel
on the water. His eyes see the wave swell in the distance, soar skyward,
bow, bend down, glide up and lick a pair of feet. A man's feet, but not
his. Bare feet, but not his, pants rolled knee-high, and higher still, keeping time to the song of the waves, a voice that wants to know what he's
doing.

"I'm following them."

"What, your dreams?"

"No, the waves."

"You want to go over there too?"

"Just looking."

"Sbania?"

"The sea."

"Look long enough and you won't be able to see anything else. That's
how she hooks you, you know."

A moment's silence, if silence is the right word for describing the
noise of the sea.

"I heard you're doing a little business."

"I buy and sell."

"Cigarettes?"

No. But with his head only. Mouth closed. Leaving the words un-
opened. All of them.

Wind. A match, a second, a third.

Smell of sulfur, then tobacco, and also, from time to time, the smell of the sea. A hand holding a mirror, and inside, Omar's face.

"You know who this is?"

"Me."

"Look closer."

"Me. Closer."

"No, a man who's going to be rich."

The hand puts the mirror in a bag, dives into a pants pocket, then opens slowly, softly as if to display something precious. But it's just grass. Grass and nothing else.

"Check it out."

Only the silence is speaking just now. For one, two, three, four, five, six seconds.

"You know what this is?"

"Trouble."

"Take a good look."

"Big trouble."

"No, asshole. It's money. Big money."

"What I said—big trouble."

"Do you have any idea what this stuff can bring on the other side, minimum?"

"Two years inside, maybe three."

Omar says nothing further. He lifts his gaze, not a bird left in the sky. Then, he turns his back on the sea and the voice, increasingly remote, the voice of one who twenty-two days, six hours, and thirty-seven minutes later was to get on a wooden boat bound for death.

31

L et's take it again from the top.

Two or three little clouds in a sky no longer entirely blue, very small the clouds, to show it's blue enough, something like the sea with its clouds of froth carried on the waves, and against the blue, and at times against the white of the clouds, a bird whose wings float with the grace of waves, as if to say that since the advent of airplanes and boats, there are fish that swim in the sky and birds that fly in the sea, and to illustrate, how many men have traveled in the sky only to wind up in the sea and how many have gone to sea only to wind up in the sky. And on the sand, a man watching the sea, *filled with wind, his shirt has the look of a gray sail*—that's the way it's written, not otherwise—as if contained in that image he's dressed in are the means to head out to the open sea. Will he respond to the sea's call? Will he yield to temptation? The more curious among us may be wondering. As for the rest, they are content to wait, as Omar himself is doing, even if one still isn't sure this concerns Omar (those who have followed closely so far will have figured it out), otherwise why would it say *a man* and not *Omar*, but in any case, there's got to be someone to keep watch on things, those waves bowing, bending down, gliding up to lick the feet. And just then you tell yourself that in the first place, it would take a tongue to lick someone's feet, and it's then you recall having read something like *the waves are that too, the sea's face leaning toward you*, so you end up conceding (because you've got better things to move on to) that if a wave is the sea's face, then it ought to have a mouth with a tongue inside with which to lick Omar's feet, Omar, who watches the waves go and come back again. And here we begin to reminisce: still small children, knees on the wet sand, hands striving to build a castle that the sea will simply take right back from us, that we'll rebuild for the pleasure of seeing her carry it off with all our work and effort. Whole minutes building what the sea will come and destroy with one flick of the tongue, and afterwards you tell yourself, "All that just for this!" already understanding, there on the beach of your childhood, the perpetual renewal of things, life a game we no longer find entertaining, a game we can't stop anymore, compelled as we are to play it. You tell yourself as well that if these waves dancing a step forward, a step back, a step forward, a step back, back and forth, never stopping, you wonder whether these waves are doing their bit in Omar's head, putting on a show in his head alone, it's there and not someplace else they hesitate, even if that isn't necessarily it exactly and even if *hesitate* isn't the best word to refer to that longing he has to go over there while staying here. And here come the waves all over again to lick men's feet with their tongues of foam, but not just his this time. Four feet in all, far too many for just one man, who wouldn't be on all fours and would consequently not be the only one there contemplating the sea. One needs only hear that voice, and not his, slipping sulfur-smelling words in your ear. And one well knows there are words that can be struck like a match, that burn if they're not put out in time. Omar is well aware of this, Omar who answers halfway, never all the way, to avoid getting burned. He answers in pieces of sentences, sometimes single words, and it is worth noting too that his answers resemble something closer to silence than to speech, so that the questions and answers never meet, something like the waves, the questions coming, the answers going. Never the same direction. He knows the thread of words ends by weaving the friendship he wants to break forever. You'll also have noticed how he says *No*, but using his head only, mouth closed, so the other can't read the words buried in his mouth. He looks at the mirror held out to him with his face inside, though he doesn't need that to recognize himself, not with all the time he's spent looking at the sea. There's no bigger mirror than the sea. Big enough, at any rate, that the whole sky can look at itself, and say what you want, that's nothing to sniff at. Before answering, Omar at times allows the silence to speak since he knows that it will get the last word anyhow. Just look at what's happening to Charaf, for he's really the one this is concerned with. His name isn't mentioned anywhere, but it's him all right, you just need to read the line again where it talks about that weed that brings in the money, big money, save for assholes like Omar. It's right there in the text "*No, asshole. Money. Big money.*" Yes, it's Charaf all right, you figure that out towards the end, not before, it would be a waste otherwise, you'd be missing something big. Charaf then, it's him all right, he's going to die, and die for real, and let it be said in passing, you can't die unless it's for real. You don't see anybody referring to a false death the way they would to false teeth that don't belong to us and are just pretending to fill up our mouths. Death belongs to us, she's there waiting from the start, and if it's been stated that Charaf is going to die, it's not just for effect, not to make the story more engaging, not even to wring a few cheap tears. If it's stated that Charaf is going to die that's because he truly is. Close his eyes for good. Not merely go off for a snooze, not just a matter of taking a breather. No, there aren't any half tones with death, it turns straight black. You never die halfway, probably to spare your having to watch the other half die. As Charaf well knows, Charaf, who's going to die all-the-way that night, who's going to be "snuffed out", as the saying goes. All one's life trying to stay lit, and along comes the sea—and it goes without saying, the sea's a whole lot of water at once—along comes the sea to snuff him out for good. The fact that he died is even there in black and white, since black is strongly preferred for announcing such things, better than white which one wouldn't necessarily see (even less so on white), and better than the color in a film that would not be in black and white. Of course, it isn't stated that he's going to die, only that he's going to *get on a boat bound for death*, which is another way, no less beautiful, no less straightforward, of saying he's going to drown, and then as well, to die. Unless we come back from that journey that is still generally termed the last. And that's when you realize you're involved in a book and not the cinema (in the first place, because there's no screen, no ticket, nobody in back of you showing off to his girlfriend, telling her the sequel to the film he's already seen) because one's going to have to be content with words such as *get on a boat bound for death* in order to understand that Charaf is going to die. And not a single drum roll to herald the event, no music whatsoever to accompany the moment, which may seem trivial to whoever's seen worse, nonetheless essential to the one leaving his life behind, considering there's only the one. It's not like the actors in those films where people get killed right and left and everybody's horsing around with death, and I'll kill you and you can go ahead and kill me next film. And yet it would be very appealing to leave this story the way one leaves a film, saddened but with the consolation—and no mean thing that, no mean thing at all—the consolation that it's only a film after all, and that if we felt like it we could have stopped the picture just by hitting a button. Just before our characters get on board that damned old tub, let's say, so it would have stayed on dry land with all those men to tug and push, the moon to keep watch, the sand to hold it back, and it not moving forward an inch without our finger's permission. But that's the thing, you don't cheat with a book, what's written is written. And perhaps we would do well to recall this phrase in connection to Charaf, since he's still the one concerned. The one who *twenty-two days, six hours, and thirty-seven minutes later was to board a wooden boat bound for death.* Thus it's written. Why *thirty-seven*, why not thirty-eight minutes later? Because that's the exact time he must drown in the book. Not drown in the words in the middle of all these pages. No, *thirty-seven* is the minute at which he must die. If it's any consolation to him, let's remember that he won't be the only one to die this way, since there's Jaafar too who's going to die and Ridouane too and Slim too and Moulay Abslam too and Louafi too and Chama too and the list is long and will stay open for whoever else might try to get their name on it someday. And for a long time still to come. So long as there's a here and a there. And the sea in between. So long as there's an over there. On the other side of the sea. And if there's no music, and no drumroll to accompany all this, no screen and no ticket either, it's in order to say that for all those drowned souls on the sand, say what you will, this isn't Hollywood.

ABOUT THE AUTHOR

Youssouf Amine Elalamy, popularly known in Morocco as "YAE," was born in 1961 in Larache, Morocco. He is a visual artist and an author of novels in both French and Darija (Moroccan dialectical Arabic). His novels include: *Un Marocain à New York* (1998), *Les Clandestins* (2000), *Paris mon bled* (2002), *Miniatures* (2004), and *Tqarqib Ennab* (2006), the first narrative ever published in Moroccan dialect. His new novel, *Nomade*, will be "published on" a city rather than in book form, turning cities into giant urban books in Rotterdam (The Netherlands) and Marrakech (Morocco).

In September 2003, Elalamy published the *Journal of YAE*, a collection of articles inspired by the terrorist attacks of Casablanca (16 May 2003). Elalamy's books have been translated into Arabic, English, Spanish, Italian, and *Les Clandestins* is currently being translated into German (forthcoming 2008). His book *Tqarqib Ennab* was adapted to the stage. *Miniatures* was exhibited as an art exposition at the Villa des Arts (Casablanca) in February 2005, as well as at other art galleries in Fes, Marrakech, Oujda and Kenitra, Morocco. Elalamy's new art exhibit, *Miniatures 2*, was held in January 2007 at the Free Academy of Visual Arts in The Hague, Holland and in June 2007 at the De Levante Art gallery in Amsterdam. His most recent exposition, "Ma Planète" (My Planet, June–September 2008), is on display at the Lydec, the central water and sanitation commission of Casablanca. The expo focuses on generating awareness particularly among young people about pollution in order to encourage recycling and resource conservation. Hundreds of school-aged children have visited the expo thus far.

In 1991, YAE was awarded a Fulbright scholarship to study the discourse of advertising in the USA. During his stay in New York City, he was affiliated with NYU (The New York Institute for the Humanities), and took courses on advertising, copywriting, and advertising layout techniques at the Fashion Institute of Technology and the Parsons School of Design. After 3 years of study in New York, he returned to live in Rabat, Morocco, where he published his first book, *A Moroccan in New York* and completed his PhD, writing a dissertation on Moroccan women's fashion magazines entitled: *Re-fashioning Women: Representation and Ideology in Moroccan Francophone Women's Magazines (Femmes du Maroc and Citadine as a Case Study)* (2004). Elalamy is the winner of the Grand Atlas Prize 2001 for his novel *Les Clandestins* and also a recipient of the British Council International Literature Prize (1999, category: travel writing). Currently, Elalamy is a founding member and on the board of the Moroccan Pen Club. He lives in Rabat with his family and is a professor at Ibn Tofaïl University in Kenitra, Morocco where he teaches Communication and Media Studies.

www.ingramcontent.com/pod-product-compliance
Lightning Source LLC
Chambersburg PA
CBHW030649110726
47901CB00002B/638